scout

scout

CHRISTINE FORD

DELACORTE PRESS

Published by
Delacorte Press
an imprint of
Random House Children's Books
a division of Random House, Inc.
New York

Visit us on the Web! www.randomhouse.com/kids
Educators and librarians, for a variety of teaching tools, visit us at
www.randomhouse.com/teachers

Library of Congress Cataloging-in-Publication Data

Ford, Christine.
  Scout / Christine Ford.
    p. cm.
  Summary: After her mother dies, eleven-year-old Cecelia befriends a new boy
at school, but soon realizes that the scruffy youth's home life is the reason for his
introspective personality, which is so much like her own.
  ISBN 0-385-73234-1 (trade) — ISBN 0-385-90260-3 (Gibraltar lib. bdg.)
[1. Friendship—Fiction. 2. Family problems—Fiction. 3. Family life—Texas—
Fiction. 4. Texas—Fiction.] I. Title.
  PZ7.F752346Sco 2006
  [Fic]—dc22   2005005696

The text of this book is set in 13-point Fournier MT Regular.
Book design by Trish P. Watts
Printed in the United States of America
March 2006
10 9 8 7 6 5 4 3 2 1
BVG

To my sons, John Paul, David, and Matthew,
for their kind help with creating this book,
and a special thanks to my daughter, Whitney,
for lending me her muse

poem has a lot of love in it.
You read it and it does something to you,
because what you are feeling
is there on the paper
and in your own heart, too.

It's like finding my Easter basket this morning,
behind the red chair.
Pop put it there.

He is in the far garden
where he goes now since Mom passed on,
every morning he goes,
Easter or no.

But I know when he put this basket together
with this purple Easter grass,
these yellow chicks

with the little brown eyes and curvy beaks,
the brilliant green pen
and notepad for making my poems,
his heart would feel the same
when hiding it as mine does finding it.

For just then,
we are the same,
Pop and me.

Love, it's a lot like that.

But there is something else I found out,
not like love at all,
and so unlike Sis,
who is on the top stair yawning,
smiling down at me,
"Pepe hasn't licked the chocolate eggs this year, has he?"
Her eyes going for her basket.
"No, not a one," I say.
Sis is just a minute searching,
long enough now we are older,
she sixteen, me eleven,
we like to look for our baskets
but not like when we were littler.

And because it is Easter Sunday
Auntie Lidia and Uncle Troy
come by bringing with them
corn relish, half a smoked ham,
spice cupcakes with buttermilk frosting,
and their boy, my cousin Aldo.
A cousin who comes in the kitchen door chomping
on a long piece of straw.

He still wears the 3-D Space Specs
that he has worn the last two times I've seen him.
Ever since in a science magazine
he spied planet Saturn behind Jupiter.
"Look," he said. "Behind that fat planet.
I couldn't even see it."
It got by him without the glasses.
After that he wouldn't take them off.

"Hey, Aldo," I say, right away being polite,
which is my first mistake because
polite or not he comes up to me,
the top of his frizzy head under my chin,
hands on hips, and says in his squeaky-brakes
kind of voice, "Who *are* you?"

And I know, even though Aldo is a shrimp for a nine-
    year-old,
and even though he has only enough friends to count
on one hand, not counting the thumb and pinky,
and the ring finger is in doubt (meaning two that I know of).
He gets a bull's-eye with me every time.

It's like I don't see the arrow coming.
He fools me because he has dimples and freckles
and he's kind of cute,
in the way of a Jack Russell terrier,
so I don't see it,
his bite.
And then, ugh,
he's got me with a joke, a trick
no one else in all the world would ever fall for.

Like the time he told me bean sprouts were like little worms
and I could use them for fishing.
Which I did.
I even began growing them in Pop's garden,
watering them every day with my blue watering can,
imagining little sprouts I could pick for fishing
instead of going nightcrawling

and digging by the light of my flashlight
for a big, clumsy worm.
Yup, I believed it.

Then the time Aldo said Yvette Carne,
a girl I admired,
dove into Quarry Lake.
I imagined her diving
in her lime tank suit
like a dart
into the murky water of Quarry Lake.
Next time I saw Yvette,
I told her, "I am going to jump. Just like you."
I said it bold-faced and up close.
So when she said, "That water's dirty! I would never do
    that."
I shrank back wordless.

And do you think I would get it with him, even now?
A cousin who knows very well who I am?

"Hey, are you listenin'?" he squeals. "Who *are* you?"

What I think to say
are those words from the poem,

"I'm Nobody! Who are you?"
The poem I was told to read aloud
in my reading-readiness class.

But I don't want to be nobody,
because for a long time now
I have not known who it is I am
or what I am supposed to be doing.

It is like being lost.
Being lost with nobody to tell it to.
Because who would listen now?
So I don't say a word.

And maybe it is because Aldo knows this,
my secret weakness, he takes the jab.
"You're just a girl."

Not Yvette Carne with the long black hair,
tan so wild she looks native,
and black, black eyes.

I drop the table talk,
march out onto the cool porch steps,
and bend down letting Pepe

just lick my nose and pow!
I kiss him. Like that.
I stretch way back so's my hair hangs way low
and call out, "Anybody here besides me?"
It is a game I play when I first come to a place.
I call out, and then I stand there listening,
letting it all—
the wind, the leaves,
the birds—have their say.
I start running up the path
till I feel the dirt at the back of my ankles.
I flop down creekside, kicking sand up everywhere.
It sounds like a laugh when it hits the water.
I laugh, too,
bringing my knees to my chest,
hugging all of me.
Cecelia Laugh Out Loud Lion. Who are you?

I am a spy train, moving through wild roses,
chasing squirrels, smudging raccoon prints,
digging in hollowed-out trees, feeling for acorns,
peeking out from behind a spotted
and gnarled old tree. Crick, creek go the vines.
Oh my crackity old bones.

And I just find the wooden bridge. Thruuump.
It makes a hollow sound when I jump.
I stand there like a scout.
Because in these woods it's all different.
I am different.
The watchman.
The lookout.
And that is why,
because I have heard my friend's little sigh,
and know he is hiding,
I hitch a vine under my arm,
take a running start,
and go out over the creek calling,
"Anybody here besides me?"
"Nope."
"That you? Come out here!"
"Yep," and then he is running at me,
grabbing the vine, our hands just touching
so's I don't even feel the weight of him
as we fly off that thrumpity bridge
heading straight into the noonday sun.

I stumble back onto the bridge,
not sure of my footing,
holding on to him.

Only I am the scout.
In these woods
I mark the trails,
watch for trouble,
make my way
like an Indian scout
with roots of the Kiowa,
learned and adopted by me
since fourth-grade history class.
So I give Redbud a little push so's he won't know
I needed that help standing up.

As usual he won't notice the push.
Just stomps his feet on the bridge,
his footfalls loud as jays.
Then we are drumming our open mouths,
circling the bridge like turkey vultures,
tighter and tighter.
And I know I am too old for this,
but like Peter Pan
I won't grow up. I won't.
And so long as I meet my friend in these woods
I never have to.
Because in these woods it's magic,
don't you know.

Finally we fall on the ground,
our heads butting, too dizzy to move.
I lie there breathing hard, trying to keep from asking.
It takes a minute but I do ask it,
the same dumb question Aldo asked me.
"Who do you think you are?"
But I know who this boy is like I know my own
    heartbeat.

His name is Redbud.
His head is shaved
so only his blond scalp shines.
He wears the same brown T-shirt
he's worn every Sunday afternoon
I've known him for the past four months,
and the same baggy, tan shorts
held up, not with a boy's belt,
but a cord, a cord cut from a matching set of blue blinds.
He has a mark, like a star,
between his pale blue eyes.
And he is named
after the Redbud tree,
a tree with purply-red blossoms,

that open sometimes before
the threat of ice
has left Texas.
Or sometimes those blossoms don't open
but wait for that warm spring day,
like the day he was born.
When, he told me,
his mother looked
out the window
saw them bloom,
"Really bloom!"
he said.
"She watched them fold open,
told my dad,
then died
three days after
with me in her arms."

As if he has not heard me ask who he is,
Redbud is lying on a bridge that is curved like
a caterpillar's back, hugging it really,
his whole arm up to his armpit in the water,
feeling for catfish.
"Do you want something to bite you?" I ask,

"Pop says cottonmouths lie low in places like that.
It's time to make tracks, Buddy."
Buddy being what I call him sometimes.

But he is still stirring up the green slime.
He stirs and stirs on
like I didn't even try to warn him.

It scares me a little when we play Robin Hood,
that serious look he gets,
when I pretend to be shot by an arrow,
him pulling me up, not even laughing,
but brushing the dirt from my shoulder,
looking into my eyes to see if I really am hurt.
When I jump up and run off,
he laughs too, and runs after me,
but it is something else.
Something that is in him
that makes that mark on his forehead
stand out like a star.

Next we scale the caprock
pretending it is a steep stone wall
of a Scottish castle,

wanting to rescue something, someone.
But we don't have that something
or even a damsel in distress,
and I won't do it for no other reason
than I don't trust him to rescue me.
Because it's only the truth.
He might spy a butterfly
and follow it.
Or hear a bird chirp and look on up to spy it.
Or see a leaf fall and try to catch it.

Redbud is the most honest person I know.
And that's good,
but it does not get me rescued
from a burning tower.
"Hey, we can rescue this."
And he points at a stubby tree with a stick
in the way Ms. Oates, my teacher, has of
pointing at the chalkboard with her pointer.
Click, click, click.

"But after we free that tree," I say,
"Let's tie that evil king up,
lock him in the tower."

I jab my stick at a tree stump
like Zorro does.
I jab like I am jabbing a man's heart.

But Redbud says
we have to bow before the evil king.
"You'll see," he says,
"that king will be so surprised
he will lay gold in our laps."

It makes sense out here
where we are like fairies in this wet place
surrounded by the lake,
and the Trinity flowing
just the other side.
And the white egrets,
you can't see them for the white sky,
and there is just water everywhere,
in our shoes, our hair, our very skin.

Then, he chases me to the swing vine,
which is deeper in the woods.
A place the sun only
peeks at now and again.

Where vines hang
sparkling from trees.
Trees that are like waterfalls.
Which is kind of funny
'cause there is no light,
least not so much
to set something to sparkle.

"What do you think?" I ask, pointing to a vine.
I grab the vine and swing out,
higher and higher, and he does not ask
how I made the vine drop.
And I wouldn't have told him
it was a trick I'd rigged
from the time before.
Instead, he calls to me, "Scout."
Not because it is my real name, it isn't.
My name is Cecelia Terwiliger.
But Scout is my woods name, his is Redbud.
Because it *is* his real name.
And because what better name than that
to have in these woods
where the Fort Worth Nature Center
is our backyard

and redbud trees grow wild
alongside paths
that keep mice, snakes, and box turtles.

I swing back, landing on the dirt path.
"What's these?" he asks,
snatching his hand from the trunk of the tree.
"Thorns," I say. And I don't guess
he has asked me this because he does
not know what a thorn is but maybe because
he is that surprised.
"Look, blood!" he says.
I watch the blood trickle up,
then tell him,
"Let's be blood brothers."
I reach for his hand,
but before I grab it he has gone and sucked
all his blood clean off his thumb.
I look at that thumb to see if there is even
a speck of blood left, but all I see is his
dirty fingernail, and not yesterday's dirt, either.
And I want to take Ivory soap and sponge his hands
    clean.
"My thumb hurts," he says, and just all of a sudden,

I can feel that hurt, too, like another's hurt, my mother's
    maybe . . .
and I don't want to be blood brothers anymore.
"Let's do it this way," I say.
I grip his hand hard.
"By the ghosts of our ancestors I swear."
"I swear," he says, after I nudge him with my
    elbow.
"To be true to the other."
"To be true," he says.
"And never to let fly with the first arrow,
or say 'give' till the last arrow's struck,
but to die with a smile."
Redbud doesn't smile.
His eyes grow wide.
He stares off as if thinking on something.
I pat him on the back.
"Now we're just like blood brothers, same as kin."
Until the light between the trees is pink.
"I have to go," I say. "Tonight it's our Easter ham and
    brisket."
When he says he is having ham and brisket, too,
I tell him he is lying.
I don't know why I say it.

Except, how could a kid like him,
scrawny as he is, be eating the same meals as me.
I sneak a look at him.
I don't like looking into hurt.
We both know he lied,
but we also know not to say it.
It is a rule.
The law of Robin and his Merry Men,
who steal from the rich to give to the poor.
Because of the Sheriff of Nottingham,
taking and using it all up.
"Those poor townspeople are starving!" he told me.
And there is something about that,
his fury at such injustice.
You just know he'd die before
he would let one of those people starve.
And there is something about that, too.
A person who would die for you, I mean.

I look out on the river.
A gull flies over the marsh.
A breeze creeps up on my skin, like bug feet.
I brush it away with my hand,
I will make it up to him.

I think then to ask him home to our Easter dinner,
but then I remember Aldo is there.
I don't want mouthy, sneaky-skinned Aldo anywhere
    near
Redbud. If I am easy, weak-kneed,
what could Aldo do to Redbud?
Honest, loving Redbud. Pitiful.

I say, "Come to dinner with me tomorrow night.
Leftovers are best."
He smiles at first, then laughs. A big laugh.
"What!" he shouts. When there is no need to
    shout.
We could hear an ant hiccup on this dock.
"And miss my mutton?" he yells.
"Mutton," I shoot back. "You eat mutton?"
"Yup," and he rubs his hard little belly.
"Lamb chop so big it takes my two
brothers to stab it and haul it to the table."
His two brothers
are imaginary, like Little John.

"Maybe," I say, sneaking it out. My eyes level
on his. "I could come to your place."

And even though Redbud and I have been friends
ever since he started
at my school after Christmas,
I have never seen his home, ever.
I don't even know if he has a real home.
Some kids at school say he lives in a spooky mansion
off of Jacksboro Highway.

Then he spoons the words out one by one.
"Maybe, I doubt it, though.
You've never seen a place like mine before.
You think my name is weird.
A girl like you, that has never even seen a place
   like mine,
you would have to be so big.
You would have to have the heart of a lion."
"I do," I say. I puff out my chest the way I see boys do,
and hope he is fooled.
Because sometimes I am not so brave,
sometimes I am yella.
Like the time I kneed, elbowed, and scratched my way
up that live oak tree to keep that dog
from using my leg for a ham bone.
I wasn't brave that day

sitting on the fourth branch
of the old oak
with everything all right,
my arms, my cheek,
everything but my self-respect.
My first tree I ever climbed
and all because I was yella.

But now I tell him, "C'mon.
I'm tough as tar, more wiry than a weed."
I shoot pebble-hard bean seeds at his skinny chest.
He swats them like they are no more than flies.
Then he touches my wrist, his eyes on mine.
"Tonight. After the world is asleep.
Meet me by the triple-trunk tree.
You want to know where I live. I'll show you."

oving from under my quilt,
trying not to make a creak
or have my sweaty toes stick like tape
to the wood floor, I tiptoe into the hall.
I hear the downstairs clock tick twice,
the railing in front of me creak
without me even near it.
I smell the apples from the kitchen sink,
where my sister set them to dry.
Funny how you can know everything
like that about a house at night,
when in the day it's like seeing through binoculars,
you only see what's in front of you,
like sugar donuts on the kitchen counter,
the waiting school bus,
and Carol Larsen at lunch
with her bunched-up red hair.
I tiptoe back to my room,
put on black shorts and a navy T-shirt,

then scuff on a pair of running shoes,
and grabbing my Halloween flashlight,
(one of those orange ones that's more
for looking in candy bags than anything else)
I head out again,
past Pop's door and Sis's,
past Pepe asleep at the top of the stairs.
How did Pepe know it was me and not something else?
If so much as a twig snapped outside
he'd make a round of barks and yips,
but I slip past him,
down the steps and out the door,
without a sound passing his mouth.
I set out, stabbing my toe on a stump
first thing off the porch.
This flashlight scares me more than it helps.
White light flashing on grass and weeds,
making it all look like I was on another planet,
maybe Mars where the light glowed.

The moon it is like a candle
between the trees, the light there,
then here, where I am
and then I see him.
Redbud, coming out of the woods

with the fog of the river bottom around him,
and the moon shining just above his blond hair.

We head out.
Me following him close enough so's
I can grab his fingers if I need to.
Close enough, I think I can smell him.
For sure I can hear his breathing, and short, soft coughs.
I am being led and I don't like it,
because I am the leader, the scout.
I watch over this wiry kid.
I keep him safe behind me.
But now at a near-run through these woods
it's turned around and here I am
behind him headed straight
at what looks to be tree trunks, bushes,
headed straight for them,
but then like a bear that knows,
his head up sniffing,
Redbud sets out at a full run
going the right way.

Flicking on my flashlight, ahead I see it.
The log that looks like the head of a giant buffalo.
Two branches stick out of the top

like horns on the buffalo's head.
Before, I would have turned
and walked the way of the river,
but tonight with Redbud,
we crawl into that tree trunk,
the mouth of the buffalo.
I am so scared my scalp tingles,
and my hair doesn't just stand on end, it screams.
The vines tangle me up, holding me prisoner.
I am trapped, I want to yell,
but like in a bad dream nothing will come out.
Redbud grabs back to get my hand.
He drags me on past it all,
the dirt, the rocks, the dark,
but most of all the stink.
It stinks in here, in this giant log,
it stinks like something dead.
Maybe just rotted green stuff,
grass, leaves, or rotted bugs, and lizards.
"C'mon. Just a little farther," Redbud says.
He has let go of my hand now,
so I grab on to his pant leg and hold tight,
and whatever I was scared of is over.
I do what he tells me.
It happens in a minute

like a push from a water slide,
before I know to be scared.
We fall from the ground,
the earth opening up and swallowing us.
We land in straw soaked with water.
Dirt sprays on my head and arms.
In front of us is a tunnel.
"Where does it lead?" I ask, all out of breath,
ready to follow him, to do what I need to do
to find his home.
It's like he's a tree elf.
Secret. Special.
I want to be a part of it.

"My house," he says.
I can't see all of him yet.
But it is high enough in here I can stand.
And I see a little shadow leading me.
Not in a hurry anymore, but fast enough,
through water that is not stinky.
Maybe river water.
"Are we in the sewer?" I ask,
sloshing on.
My feet feel gluey inside my soaking shoes.
"Maybe," he says, and I want to hit him for that,

because he knows. He has done this before.
There is enough light now to see the back of his head.
The little pieces of yellow straw in his hair, stuck there,
    like flies to flypaper.
It is getting lighter all the time.
I hear stomping above us.
Echoes string along the tunnel walls like tinkling glass.
The sewer walls seem to shrink with the sound.
And all around us straw is falling like snow.
I don't know where we are.
I am walking in a sewer listening.
Listening for what?
What does a scout listen for?

"Not so far now," he calls back.
It is all so soft.
The light is like a candle.
First here, then there.
I think of the moon.
"Redbud," I call.
I don't see him ahead anymore,
and then I don't hear
his sloshing feet.

He is first out of the tunnel.
After hitching one foot after the other in cracks
along the sides.
I do just like him till we are in a hallway
that is darker, colder than the tunnel.

It leads to a stairway.
"C'mon," he calls, racing far ahead of me.
"Why'd you stop?"
"I didn't," I say, "I'm coming."
I run down the hall after him.
"C'mon." He puts out his hand for me.
I take it and race up the stairs with him.
Out of breath, climbing the stairs,
and it is darker here than in the tunnel.
My arms are cold.
I have goose bumps down to my wet feet.
It is that cold with air-conditioning.
It smells of cherry juice and that stuff Pop uses
to clean the kitchen floor.

Redbud's hand is sweaty in mine.
We are in a kitchen.
The light over the sink is on.

We round a long yellow countertop,
turn into a green room
with a brown couch against a far wall.
Toys hang out of a toy box in one corner.
Stepping over a dump truck,
I land on a plastic ball that squeaks.
He pushes me in a hall closet.
"What are you doing? Don't you live here?" I ask.
"Yes. I don't want them to see me.
They told me I couldn't go out.
The nurse said I was too sick."
"So tell them you're better," I say.
I don't like the smell of this closet,
and I don't need to see to know
that it is filled with moldy mops and dusty pails.
"That doesn't work around here," he says.
He doesn't seem to smell the mops.
And then I think to ask it.
"You have your own nurse?"
"The home does," he says.
"The home?" And I don't want to know any more
because I don't want all this mystery
to grow into something I'll hate.
Something not secret or special,

but something ordinary and hurtful.
"Yes," he whispers, "Sara Church Home.
Where we are now."
Sara Church Home.
I have heard that name before,
but where I don't know.
It doesn't sound ordinary, though.

He leads me out of the closet, climbing more steps,
Redbud's finger to his lips shushing me past the lady
guarding bedtime in a long dark dress
and black boots rocking slowly in a chair.
I look past her to see two rows of beds along opposite
    walls.
Blankets are crushed in corners,
tossed over bedposts,
and onto the floor.
Some are smooth
over kids' bare legs.
I squeeze Redbud's hand harder.
We round the corner,
race down three flights of steps,
past a security guard,
and out the back door.

I breathe clean air
asking between breaths
if they know he is missing.

"Not yet, I guess," he says.
"And what if they find out?" I say,
looking at his face,
that pale, skinny face.
The sickness,
the smell, too, familiar.
He says, "Nothing much.
I leave at mealtimes so's they don't miss me.
No attendance taken then. I might miss a meal, but that's all."
And I wonder how many dinners
he has missed on account of meeting me out in the
    woods.
"I don't get hungry like most kids," he says.
He takes a dive into the field, running.
I run after him, calling,
"Do you want to get lost?"
"Don't you think I know where we are?" he says.
"I can see in the dark, silly.
It's not really dark,
just another color like purple.
Everything looks different in purple,

but once you get used to it, it is just dark."
I laugh. This kid is great.
We run into the great, great purple night.

Next day, Pop has left for the far garden.
His yellow birds,
all he makes anymore,
flutter in the garden sky
on thread-thin metal.
They flutter like real birds made of feathers,
but made with metal and painted
to look like fine feathers.

Before Mom died he made all sorts of things,
striped metal cats, owls, zany clocks,
googly-eyed lizards, fun things.
Now the yellow birds.
This yellow that he matched from a peony.
Since my mom died
color is all he notices.
Certainly not me.

My sister in her noisy car has gone
a couple minutes before.
The thought clicks, up past midnight

and no one has found me out!
I am up and out of bed
dancing what I think is the jitterbug
in the parlor to music I think is jitterbug music.
Cat is curled up on the sofa.
A big grin on her brown face.
The red poppy on the windowsill
(the one in a clay pot my sister has painted green)
bounces to the beat I stamp out on the floor.
I spot Sis's magazine on the TV.
A poem to Eddie is there, too.
Eddie is her boyfriend going on a year now.
Sis 'n' Eddie, like the front and back sides of a good
    book.

I pick the poem up to read.

My life
Never meant so much
To me
Till there was you
To walk with me,
Talk with me,
To just be
Here with me.

I can do better than that.
I pick up the pen and pad lying beside the magazine.

To Eddie

My curly kinky hair never meant so much to me
Till there was you to pull it.
My big nose never meant so much to me
Till there was you to blow it.
My big mouth never meant so much to me
Till there was you to kiss it!

By Sis 'n' Eddie

Much better.
In the kitchen
I go from cupboard to cupboard
grabbing the Breakfast O's,
the sugar, and a bowl.
I sniff in the sunshine pouring in from the windows.
The outdoors is waiting for me to drink up my milk
and race out the back to shake Pepe up.

Which I do.
Pepe paws my pajama shirt

till I fall back onto Sis's old bed
that is out here on the porch,
for no other reason, Pop says,
than to get it out of the way.
"Birds! Pepe," I say.
I need to feed the birds,
water Pop's herbs,
watch that toad hop out of the oregano,
and just touch the silver beetle
that is like a raindrop in the dark dirt.
I pump water from the well,
whistle to the mockingbird
overhead in the pine tree,
thinking of Redbud.
Where he is right now,
and would they let him out?

What would it be like to never taste
the well-water mornings,
follow a beetle with your eyes,
or hear a mockingbird?
Because how could you with adults
yammering,
bells going off all the time,
people worrying,

will these kids ever get it?
And then lunch
and cherry juice.
Maybe you could, still.
Maybe Redbud did.
Heard a bird, I mean.

Today, though,
I will not go look for Redbud.
I will ride my bike to May's house,
where we will look at comics in her bedroom.
The bedroom with purple pufftop curtains.
The bedspread, too, purple,
And a nice white desk with
a gold drawer-knob.
Where I will find brand-new Archie comic books
stacked on a furry white rug
in the middle of her bedroom floor.

We do not like Archie.
Not just because of his looks,
but because there is something
we both like, instead, about Reggie.
And we do think Jughead is goofy and fun.

Of the two girls, I am Veronica
because of my dark hair
that flips at the shoulders just like Veronica's does.
She is Betty,
because her hair is blond
and she wears it pulled into a ponytail,
only high up on her head,
pulled so tight her eyes
are like little blue almonds.
Even though she acts like Veronica
and I act more like Betty.
Why is it we want what we don't already have?

Like I said, May is more like Veronica.
She is pretty and little
with tiny feet that I admire.
She has smooth shiny knees
(mine are dark and knobby).
She likes white,
white dresser, desk, comforter, bed lamps,
shoelaces, and Barbie in white gowns.
I like orange.
"Orange, yikes!" she says.
"Nobody actually likes orange!"

Most times, we dance, May and me,
to the boom box outside on her porch,
and make up skits that we discover in books from
her father's library, where I read
Oliver Twist, David Copperfield,
and *The Pickwick Papers.*
All leatherbound.
Where it smells
of wrapped peppermints,
rich carpet,
and lemony furniture polish.

The skits we make up are Christmas skits
about little kids who get noisy presents
and eat too much Christmas fudge.
And Independence Day skits
where we act out the fun of fireworks
with last year's sparklers
and charge twenty-five cents
to the kids on May's street.
Sometimes somebody pays,
usually a grown-up,
and then it's worth it when
we take our quarter to the
Mobil and buy sour balls

that we suck on all the way home.
Suck on till we can taste our cheeks.
May and me go each year to the summer carnival,
where we win spotted stuffed animals,
buy buttered popcorn, cotton candy,
and blue bubble gum
that we blow into giant bubbles, then
take turns popping the other's
with our finger.
Poppity pop! It's a blue nose for you!

On the Ferris wheel
May giggles and tilts our seat back and forth
and my stomach feels icky,
and it's all I can do not to throw up,
and ugh I hate the tip-top on the Ferris wheel.
"Please!" I want to yell to the carnival guy
running the ride.
"Take us down now!"
But I don't.
I think he's gone to sleep against the post
and will never get me down.
And you know what?
I am going to cry or fart or burp or something.
"Get me down!"

I yell to everybody's surprise.
Even May's, and she smiles at me,
and doesn't rock anymore but grabs hold of my hand,
which I don't pull away even though I could and want to,
I don't because she is so darned nice.
But I feel so darned bad.
I am such a Ferris wheel chicken.

But May thinks I am perfect.
As long as I'm perfect with May,
I'm okay with the other kids at school,
who all think she knows something about me they don't.
I've got them fooled.
I'm just a girl with rubbery legs.

Blue

Blue is the beauty of the sky
Nice, bright and shining high

Blue is the color chosen for boys
Blue is the color of baby toys

Blue shows when you're down in the dumps
Especially with chicken pox bumps

Blue is the color of my shirt,
Which matches my striped blue skirt

Blue is the color of ink I use
And my favorite color I choose

Blue will be the color of my car
When I am a movie star

Cecelia Terwiliger

I tape my poems up after
I finish one.
Tape it to my green walls.
Two whole walls are about covered.
One poem is of the sunlight
just right,
like a lemon lollipop.
And there is another one
I wrote in the third grade
to my mom
for Mother's Day
just before she died.

Dear Mom

I love you with all my hart
You are so beautiful
It makes my hart shiver.
I dance in joy when you hug me.

Love,
Cecelia Terwiliger

That same day my mom
took me to the movies
in downtown Fort Worth,
where we saw *Raiders of the Lost Ark*.
And ate ice cream afterward,
for me, a caramel pecan sundae.
My mom's favorite was strawberry shortcake
ice cream in a cone.
Then on to Dillard's department store,
which used to be Leonard's, my mother tells me,
where downstairs,
she used to, with her aunt Carol,
buy a box of chocolates,
and just like we do now,
eat them,

one by one,
in no order at all,
mixed nut, macadamia, pecan,
dark chocolate,
a bite of coconut,
tangerine,
fudge.

All on our ride on the Tandy
which used to be the M & O Subway
back to our waiting station wagon
in the parking lot.
And drive in quiet
on the Jacksboro Highway,
drive the ten miles back into the country,
the city behind us like a kingdom.

I got a chain
in my box of Cracker Jack
from the movie.
I still have that.
Guess what?
It has a little
silver (hart) heart
dangling from it.

Picking it up off my dresser,
I can feel a tear
starting on my eyelash.
My mother is in this heart.
Dahlia Terwiliger.
I let the heart dangle for a minute,
then in a pile of blankets
in my corner of my room
I sit, with my journal,
opening it I write,

For you
Who will
Never go away
Because
Of this tear
This heart
I have for you

It is as I tuck my journal
back under the cushion
that I draw out a dog's collar.
It is made of a leathery blue and dotted
with blue rhinestones.

Pepe's collar that Sis bought
since she's been loving him too much now,
loving and buying him stuff like
a bone that smells like a vanilla cupcake,
and a dainty toenail file that does not work.
When I pick up that file to even move it,
Pepe jumps up quick and backs away.
When Sis pets him she sings
country music.
Songs like "Dang Me,"
and "Walk Through the Bottomland."
He does not like it.
Even though his eyes grow soft and wide,
and his ears perk up and his tail moves with it.
No. He likes jazzy tunes—
he's a jazzy dog.
One kind of dog for Sis
and a whole 'nother kind for me.
"Who is the real Pepe—hmmmm?"
I scruff up his fur because he is here
with me, as always at my side.

We lie here just looking at the cracks,
the curling paint of my green walls.
My mother died

two months after
I gave her that hart poem.
She died of cancer.
Not slow.
But fast enough I could not stop it.
Nor the doctors nor anyone else.
All I wanted was to stop it.
"Arrest it" is what that's called.
I tried to stop it with my weight.
I stopped eating until they told me that was what I was
    doing.
And it didn't do any good anyhow.
So I might as well have that salami sandwich
and chocolate ice cream.

Pop made things
with his garden art
after that.
Nobody wanted them.
Not even him.
Twisted shapes,
hollow and blind.
Pop said, "Death is blind.
Blind as a bat.
And it eats our insides."

I was scared then
of how hollow and blind and
all eaten up Pop appeared.
Not even like my real pop anymore.

So I wonder how
Redbud must feel
with no mom
and where is his dad?
I wonder if he feels anything like Oliver Twist.
Or David Copperfield,
who smack in the middle of London
had nobody to look at him.

Then, shaking the blues out,
I race Pepe
for the door
and down the stairs
to go to the river and fish, yes!

To the porch,
swinging the screen door almost inside out,
I race to the shed to get my fish pole,
tackle box, and then back again,
in the kitchen scratching

scratching, scratching
to the back of the icebox
for hot dogs,
and pieces of bologna for bait.
I am out the door
charging down the path
Pepe at my heels barking.
What for? Happy again.
That's why. Happy.

But the fish aren't biting.
It is hot.
I got bug bites,
and my hair is all snarly
the way Pop hates,
and no sandwiches.
Down here for hours
with nothing to eat.
The brush crackles,
a turkey vulture's wings snap shut,
then a rustle of wings,
that buzzard is above me in the tree
and no matter what anybody says
turkey vulture or not
it stinks,

it's dirty,

and means death,

and I am bothered by it.

But I stay still 'cause that's the way I learned

in the woods when you're not sure

you don't move,

just like the animals,

they take that minute

to get sure.

But the sound is closer

and I figure I am no animal so

I am about to grab my pole from the water

when Redbud

climbs out of the bushes

acting like a zombie,

or what could be a zombie,

eyes crossed,

tongue hanging out,

arms out,

hands bobbing

in front of him.

I brush the mud from my knee,

"So what's doing?" I say, all brave-like,

like I wasn't even bothered a darn by any sound,

and I am not bothered now by how darned ugly he looks.

"You sneak out again?"
"Yup," he says,
dropping the zombie routine.
He walks over to the riverbank,
picks up my fish pole.
"Hey, watch it," I say,
"I could have something there."
He smiles a sly smile.

I wish I had a poem
to open it up for me.
To know what it is that smile says.
"What is on the other end of nothing is nothing,"
    he says.

This piece of grass I am twisting
I tie in a knot,
thinking, this kid is making
a knot of my thoughts.
I watch him reel in my line.
Watch, too, as he sweeps a cast
to the middle of the river.
He gives a tug to the line, then feels the line
between his thumb and forefinger,
and I wonder, did he learn that,

to feel for the fish, at the home?
I want to ask him,
where are your mom and pop?
and will you eat tonight?

Instead, I kick pebbles in the water
as he catches two catfish,
then doubles that,
and before we are ready to go,
he has nine good-sized catfish.
I rub his short, bristly hair.
It feels warm in the sun and
puts me in mind of wild honeybees,
which puts me in mind of wild-bee honey,
which puts me in mind of supper.
"Come to our fish fry.
We'll cook these up.
All of 'em at my house. C'mon now."
He digs his heel in the dirt and says, "Awww . . ."
"Pop does the catfish," I say,
"breaded in meal, fries them up in hot oil,
canned peaches sweet as butterscotch,
and we'll eat them whole
so cold,
shaped like little hearts.

C'mon. There'll be hush puppies,
and pink lemonade
back of the house,
at the pit by the shed."
He points to the biggest fish.
"Save that for me."
I say, "Yes, yes,"
as I string the fish,
and grabbing my net,
and pole,
I rise up on one knee,
to see he is already gone.

I could carry wood as fast
as Pop's song,
all jumbled and rumbly
and long.
Sweet the sound of that wood.
It pops on the fire
like the catch in Pop's throat.
Never knew where he'd leave off with a word
before another one started,
and like the fire,
catch a little quicker.
Soon we'd be smelling
panfried catfish,
on that grill Pop is sweating over,
and eating corn on the cob
that I will shuck and spill into the kettle,
and taste okra, fried okra,
which is way too slimy.
Sis would bring Eddie by,

and we'll all grab a seat and sit under
the big live oak tree
that shades it all—
the shed, the barbecue pit, the tire swing,
the old stump that is mine,
it is where I sit,
and the card table Pop has set up today for this occasion,
and I have covered with a plastic checkered tablecloth
(and set black-eyed Susans in a jelly jar in the middle),
just like my mom used to do.

And Eddie will make us laugh
with the telling of the characters
down at the auto shop,
like the man
who didn't know how
to stop his own truck.
Ran straight into a light pole.

It is six o'clock now,
but looking off
into the trees,
I don't see Redbud coming.

Would the people at the home
let him come?
Or make him eat peanut butter
on celery with raisins
like ants caught in glue.
And then I see the shine of his bristly hair
in the sun coming out of the woods.

Redbud doesn't like Pop's catfish,
and corn on the cob insults him.
It is too much for his delicate mouth,
and okra is for possum, he says,
but he does enjoy chocolate cake.
Which Sis has brought to him
on a dainty plate,
showing me she likes him enough,
even after giving me the eyeball
when I said, "Sis, here is Redbud."
Said it like I was handing her a platter of fried dough,
instead of a good friend.

He is on his fifth piece of chocolate cake
when Pop brings out the guitar.
Eddie sings along,

and for a boy who has chunky black hair
and creamy, dreamy skin
he sings the notes from somewhere deep inside him
so deep it goes deep inside me, too.
He reaches that empty spot,
the hole my mother left,
and fills it with sound.
Beautiful, sweet
sound.
Like waves on a lake.

His voice makes me want to marry him.
Oh to listen to it all day long—
at the park, school, in the car.
It gets inside you and you don't ever want the melody
    to stop.
But the music does trail off.
Pop moves on to something else.
Something slow, not too jazzy,
so we can think on what we just lost.

I am mostly happy like this.
Though I do miss Mom and how she'd look at me
and smile and I'd know we would talk after this
doing dishes at the kitchen sink.

Discuss Eddie,
and maybe laugh about Pop and how careful
he gets about catfish
and corn.
And she would probably tell me,
though I already know,
there is something about Redbud.
Not so much what he's missing.
Everybody knows that.
A good soak in the bathtub,
somebody to show him
where his belt is (oh no, that cord!)
And a mother to comb his sweet
honey-colored hair
instead of shave it like he is a sheep,
not like the lamb he is.
And that is what it is.
He is like a woolly lamb.
Sweet and soft
and sincere.
And in his sincerity,
she would say, is his strength.
And she would rinse the last dish
and unlike Pop,
who only sees the dish

he is rinsing,
she would see me in the dish
and we'd laugh
like into a mirror.

Sis 'n' Eddie start a game of checkers,
and Redbud wants more cake.
So I give it to him, the whole thing,
telling him eat it all if you like.
I like watching him eat.
His little body gobbles it up,
his head bobbing.
He looks off in the direction of the trees.
I don't think he knows,
but there is a smile,
there, I see it.
And then before I know it I am
handing him a jar of the peaches.
I tell him, take them back home for the others.

"Not going back there," he says,
"I'm going to my other home."
"Your other home?" I say.
"Yeah, I stay this weekend with my dad,"
and when he says it he is looking at the dirt in my drive.

"My caseworker says the six months are up.
She says things will be fine now and if this weekend
    works out,
I will be there from now on. You wanna come over?"
I don't want to go, but there is something
in me that does not listen.
"Sure."
"Tomorrow, then," he says.
And he is looking at me but not in the eye.
"I'll meet you at the buffalo pen
at the far side of the prairie.
Oh, and you can keep your peaches.
You'll need a cold heart."

After saying good night to Sis 'n' Eddie,
Pop is passing by my room,
outside in the hall.
"Good night, Pop."
"Ceil?"
From my doorway,
I see him look for me in the other direction.
Lives in his head, he does.
A cloud up high
and away from me.

Then he peeks in,
says, surprising me,
"You really get along, don't you?"
He means Redbud and me.
"Sure," I tell him.
"He lives close by then? His family?"
I tell him no and no.
I turn into my blanket smelling
the Downy
Pop has rinsed it in,
and eyeing my New York Yankees hat that
hangs on the bedpost.
I see again Redbud's bed.
No sheets.
No pillowcase.
I see again the same gray walls,
beds close,
but not for whispering to a friend,
but for sleep
when the bell rang.

"He lives at Sara Church Home," I tell Pop.
"Sara Church Home," he says, "you mean the place
past Turner's Farm?"
"Yes," I say.

I don't tell Pop about the other home.
Not yet.
"Oh," Pop says.
"Yes?" I say.
"Well, Ceil, that is a home boys and girls go to
when there is something wrong at home.
Sometimes the children need help is all."
"What kind of help?" I ask him.
"Getting their lives fixed up.
It is a place kids go when things have fallen apart
    at home.
A safe place."
My last thought after Pop leaves
and before I fall asleep
is that Redbud is not in that safe place tonight.

Next day I dig through my closet
till I find my yellow cotton dress.
I shake it out, dust and all,
thinking, why not?
And I put it on.
I take up the brush
with the little pearl handle,
the one my grandmother gave me
for my fifth birthday,

when she said
I had grown enough hair
to warrant using one.
After rinsing it in the sink
and getting it good and wet
I comb my bangs the way I want them,
back off my forehead.
I shake that brush hard.
Water splats this way and that,
on my phone,
a picture of Aldo
looking dumb in his 3-D Space Specs,
and a card,
bought for me by my mother
at the card shop down at the Tandy Center.
On the face of the card
is a young medieval queen,
looking out at me
as if asking a question,
no, not just asking it,
but seeking it.
She is frozen like that
with the question that I think
makes her sad.
Above her in both corners

are heads of bronze men with seaweed hair
and what look to be copper pennies for eyes,
mouths wide open.
Gargoyle gods.
Inside the card, I know without looking
what it is my mother has written there,
Cecelia, you have the heart of a jewel.
I have read that a thousand times.
But still I wonder,
what is it you expect of me, Mama?

Pop calls from outside my bedroom door,
"Cecelia, you holed up in there for a reason?"
I close the card and tuck it away in my dresser
    drawer.
"I am going to meet Redbud," I say,
"I am going to his weekend home."
"Oh?" Pop says. "Where is that?"
"On the lake," I say. "It is real nice."
"Oh?"
And it is just like Pop not to come in
and not to ask too many questions.
Sometimes I think he is experimenting
bringing me up now Mom's gone.
Experimenting. And I like the sound of the word.

"Yes," I say. "Redbud and his dad
are having an experimental weekend together
and Redbud says I can come."
I make noise like I am moving perfume bottles and
    brushes,
clinky stuff, girl stuff.
Pop does not like to mess with his experiment.
"Oh, well, then, you have a good time, Ceil," he says,
and then, "Be home by noon."
"Yes, Pop," I say.
Pop thinks nobody, no matter what he does,
can get into trouble before noon.
"And Ceil," he says from outside my door.
"Yes, Pop?"
But he says nothing.
Stillness.
"Yes, Pop?" But I am not hoping anymore,
nor guessing on what I want Pop to say.
Maybe, *I love you.*
But no, I am not waiting anymore.

May saw Redbud outside a house once
when we walked Confederate Highway, the road we
    were not supposed to be on.

The highway of speeding cars and semis
that leads to the fenced part of the nature center.
"Ugh" is what she said, when she saw the house.
I said, "The beauty is he doesn't ever have to wipe
    his feet!"
I said this not because I knew at all what went on in
    that house.
I said it because I wanted it to be true.

I took him to May's house after.
Don't know why, but sometimes
I like to put things together
that don't match
just to see what will happen.
In the same way I do in a poem.
Sometimes it surprises.
Like a good sneeze.

May does not make us wipe our feet
at the doormat,
but asks us, "If you don't mind too much—"
looking down at Redbud's sandy sneakers
with the hole at the toe,
"take those off!"

So in our stocking feet
we float in May's house.
A cloud of a house
with shiny candlesticks
and gold-looking candles
on a fireplace mantel that looks like
a ship's bow, a Viking ship
of white wood.
And windy stairs where you can stand at the bottom
in the middle and see all the way to the top.
And what a wonder,
Redbud is there looking
down at me.
His mouth an O.

Oh, oh, parents not home!
Sparking up the kitchen floors in our stocking feet,
we cross the other's path,
climb on May's bed,
her "two stories" of piled pillows.
And on her shamrock-green hall carpet,
leaving our tracks.
And that is how I finally find Redbud

under a yellow table skirt in the den
on his belly, his feet on the back wall,
so when I lift the tablecloth
he uses his feet to spring out at me,
catching one of my braids.
Ouch! Ouch! Ouch!

We both roll back to the TV spot,
which May has never left,
sucking her pinky finger
and watching Scooby-Doo.
We sink in next to her
and she shudders at Redbud
being so close.
So he crab-walks over to me,
then lets himself fall.
"Hmmmmf!"
Loud enough for
May to know he doesn't stink
or have a disease
or have a rash or something.
I smile over at him,
pat his fuzzy head.
He buries his eyes in the TV.

But I think he knows
I don't care how May is with him.
He is better than that.

During the commercials
May tootles in the kitchen,
then carries a black plastic tray
of cheese and crackers
and cherry Kool-Aid back to us.
She sets the tray down between me and where she is
    sitting,
then hands me a glass, smiling
with a sideways look at Redbud,
who looks as if he has snitched his glass.
"Don't spill!"
Which is an invite
as far as I know to spill
and he does
and May shakes her head
and squeals little squeals
at him, a brute with no manners!
And Redbud tries to help her
clean up cherry Kool-Aid
off beige carpet.

Which is impossible!
I call Pop.
Ask how to get it out
and he tells me vinegar
and so we do that
only apple vinegar's
all May's house has
and now it is an apple-smelling cherry stain.
And I drag the hall rug over it and say,
"There!"
And May has her door open for Redbud
but tries to get me to stay.
And I know how it is with her.
She is already paving the way for school.
No Redbud at our lockers,
or sitting with us in the lunchroom.
He will ruin us.
In that way he did
when we stood in line
for the home basketball game
at our gym.

He *did* know us after all,
or me, anyway, from history class,

but when I let him cut in line,
he got too excited
and told these corny jokes that I thought were so
    funny,
but no one else did,
and he laughed till he spit,
and then I laughed and we both had to sit out the game
on the gym steps because my friends gave us the cold
    shoulder that night, well, all except May.
She brought us buttered popcorn.
But the funny thing is Redbud
did not care much about missing the game,
and neither did I.
But we both wanted to hear the trumpet
and sax player in our school band.
We were real quiet then.
Letting the music swim over us.
I knew he was more like me then than anybody else
ever was or could be,
because he liked music more than one basketball game,
and he liked the night better than the day,
and he liked a girl for a friend as much as any boy.

But May does not get Redbud
to leave her house

because she is mean.
She is not.
It's only the truth.
Redbud's holey-kneed pants
and rumply sweatshirts
and sweet jelly-donut smeared
mouth and all his do-gooding
are not liked at our school
by anybody
and truth be,
if I didn't know him already,
not me, either.

Because whenever you look at Redbud
you have to ask yourself
is the sugar from my morning donut
still at the corners of my mouth?
Are these wear spots at my knees too much so
the other kids notice?
And am I being too good today—
meaning—when we finished with it, did the basketball
need to go back in the barrel where Ms. Larsky liked it
    to go?
And did we really have to say sorry to Jamie I'm-too-
    cute-for-you

for filching her Blue Goddess soap bar out of the
    shower stall?
No!
He just makes you so mad that way!

So I press May's fine-boned hand
but feel a little guilty,
a traitor to Redbud.
And so I call him
and together we follow May's
stony path to the road.

I ride my bike.
Redbud tags alongside.
And we move slow, then fast, and faster.
Then we have that free feeling
between us and we laugh,
then crash my bike
into the lilac bush,
where we sit
in front of it
for a long time
eating lemon drops
Redbud pocketed
(but first asked May for)

from the candy dish
that almost broke
when he scooped them out,
but didn't.
"You're lucky," I tell him now.
"Forty dollars!" Redbud repeats May's exclamation
at the tumbling candy dish before I caught it.
"A forty-dollar candy dish!
We could buy a bucket of fireballs with forty dollars."
"A grocery sack full," I say, playing our game.
"A wagon load."
"A Dumpster full."
"A jet plane."
"A steamboat."
And we laugh at the picture
our minds make of a steamboat full of red-hot fireballs.

When we go back to school
May will be my best friend like always.
But right now for this Easter vacation Redbud is.

It is just after a rain,
when everything is new again.
The sun on the tall prairie grass
tinting it not red but auburn.

Auburn, like my aunt Molly-who-lives-in-Ireland's hair.
And the grass in the mesquite grove
it's like Easter grass
that green cellophane kind
all shiny and bunchy with sun.
I follow two yellow butterflies
as they flit ahead of me.
Never looking down the path at all.
I sing a poem I made up in kindergarten,
"Butterfly butterfly tie my shoe,
butterfly butterfly zip my zippers,
butterfly butterfly I'll follow you,
butterfly butterfly shoo shoo shoo!"
I stop, surprised by Redbud, who
stands at the end of the path,
in front of the buffalo pen,
dressed, too warm,
in jeans and sweatshirt.

"Hi," I call.
"Come on," he says. "You're late."
I follow Redbud out of the red and gold fields
and deep into shadow,
and feel the wind die on my cheek.
We are in a gully,

our footsteps
spray up sand and dust-brown moths.
Tree roots climb ahead of us
like steps that lead to gnarled trees.
We come to a fork in the path.
Redbud takes to the left
a switchback that leads us
down to the road.
On the road we pass
empty milk cartons,
yellow newspapers,
bits of rabbit fur,
rusted paint buckets,
a plastic-bead necklace
and a pair of kid's sunglasses lost in a puddle.
We teeter-totter over beaten-down chicken wire.
I watch my new shoes get a scrape on them.
When I look up
it is to see a small gray house,
the same house May and I saw
along that highway to the nature center,
the house May pronounced, "Ugh!"
There is a rocker pitched to one side.
A skinny stand of pansies
and marigolds at the step.

Pieces of a clay flowerpot
crunch under my feet.
A Chevy pickup
is in the drive
alongside an old black Cadillac.
An old white dog
lies in the dirt, tied to a post.
"What's your dog's name?" I ask.
"Maggie," he says.
"Hey, Maggie." It comes out of me like a bird chirp.
And for the first time I know I am a little bit afraid.
We are on the stoop
and Redbud's beating up a screen door.
The screen shakes
like a rattletrap jalopy.
If it was me doing it back at my house
Pop would have guessed it was me on the
other side of an emergency.
But no sound from inside this mouse-quiet house.
The inside door creaks open as if by itself.
A tall woman in a housedress
with hair the color of wheat
comes forward
out of a shadow.
She is soft looking

like a marshmallow.
"Memaw, this here is Scout," Redbud says.
We troop past his grandmother,
and maybe because she is now holding a soupspoon
and bringing a lovely golden liquid to her mouth,
I think of my own gran, who is taller,
with elbows and knees that are sharp edges,
eyes that like to bore holes.
"Interesting" is Gran's favorite word.
"How do you do," I say.
But no words of welcome come back my way.
We file down a carpeted hall.
An orange smell is coming
from a small room on the left.
I see past the open door
into where china dolls
lie on a white fancy bedspread,
Memaw's room, I think,
a room that because the door is only open halfway
and the fresh smell of oranges is
coming from in there, I figure
she must eat in there.

We stream on past
another door

that is closed.
Cigarette smoke drifts into the hall
from somewhere.
"C'mon," he says,
because I have slowed.
I hear a rattle coming from behind that closed door,
there is scratching and whimpering.
Something is trying to get out.
"Redbud?" But he is gone, his back
to me, shoulders hunched like
no matter what, he is not going to turn around.
I want to see what it is that is now at that door, yelping.
An animal? But it has a deep growl when I get close,
so I hurry to catch up to Redbud.
Redbud just pushes his way
past a dingy door
into his room.
Paper covered in crayon,
reds, blacks, greens,
of wagons, airplanes, helicopters,
buses—they're all over his white walls.
"Going somewhere?" I say.

He shows me his collections:
rocks, birds' eggs, lures,

turtle shells and soap shavings,
all different kinds of soaps in colors
pink, green, ivory, blue.
"From everybody I know," he says.
"Soap. Smells good, don't you think?"
I do.
"But what's these?"
On his wall is a rattlesnake skin pegged to a board,
almost three feet long.
And on that same board is a scorpion still with a tail,
and a tarantula that looks almost alive.
"Where did you get this stuff?"
He stuffs his collections back into the boxes and plastic
    dishes,
then shoves them back under the bed, saying,
"My father charmed that snake.
You got to hold your gun barrel
to its head and it'll follow it.
Just like a cobra to a flute.
Then he shot it."
"He charmed it, then shot it?" I say.
"There's a frog skin. Wanna see?"
He takes from his top drawer
a box, then opens it, and
from between wax paper he lifts

a beautiful green-blue skin.
I hold it up to the light.
It has an orange glow.
A perfect frog shape,
round little belly,
and itty-bitty feet.
"Feels crisp like a fried tortilla," I say.
He nods.
Then says, "I found that by the road all dried up.
I gave it a home with me."
There is something on the dresser.
Up close I see pieces of yellow and brown glass,
but when I move back I make out
a horse's head.
A beautiful glittering horse's head.
It is like with Pop's garden art,
what looks like rusty metal up close
from far away against the blue sky
looks like something from heaven.

Then, sliding back using my toe
to trace the deep scratches in the wood floor,
I find myself sitting on Redbud's bed.
It rocks like a porch swing.
"It's what I like," he says.

He climbs next to me and we rock and rock.
We are a ship launching.
An airplane at takeoff.
A taxicab with a stuffed green monkey passenger.
Redbud and me are laughing,
rocking like this, when
we hear a sharp whistle.
Redbud sits up
like a collie that's heard a bell.
"Sergeant Major's home," he says.
Redbud is at the door.
He opens it a crack.
From down the hall,
like it is way off, we hear
"Soup bowl is cracked."
A man's voice.
And then a clatter
and a small cry.
"What is it?" I ask.
"Stay back," he says.
"Don't you come out till I come get you."
He slams the door behind him.
But I am the scout! Why am I always behind this kid?
So I hug the door, listening:
plates scrape,

pans set,
shoes cross the tiled floor.
I listen,
knowing there is an animal in another room
knowing his memaw eats by herself
in her orangey room,
knowing there is a charmed snake
pegged to a board next to me,
but no matter how much any of this makes me afraid
I tiptoe out of the room
all the way
to the end of the hall,
because I have to know what is happening out there,
and I guess, too, I have to know I can do this.
So I move into the living room behind a chair,
where I listen.

"Crackers, soldier."
And then Redbud. "Yes, sir."
"And them cookies, too.
Bring some of those.
What they called, Mother?"
"Gingersnaps, Major," says Memaw.
"Hop to it, boy." A voice snarly and loud.
"Bring that whole bag over here."

"Yes, sir."
And then I am not behind the chair
because I need to get a better look
and next I know—
"Well, what have we here?" I see him stand up
from the far end of the kitchen table.
"A possum that's sneaked its way in our house.
And wearin' a pretty dress, too."
I curtsy. I don't know why.
Maybe the "pretty dress."
"This possum's polite. Come here, girl.
Come on over here."
I do, and stand looking up at him.
I see his wide shoulders,
the T-shirt with the small hole at the right shoulder,
lips almost white over straight white teeth.
He has a tan, tan face and a crew cut
of the same wheat-color hair as Redbud's memaw.
His jaw is wide, a dimple like
a raisin in the middle of his chin,
eyes like what gold dust must be
shining light on everything.
"Set it up, soldier!"
My foot hits the table leg at that,
like when Dr. Baird checks my reflexes in her office.

It's because he has yelled so loud.
Redbud, like a rabbit to a hole,
sets the table with green beans,
grabs a fork and spoon from Memaw,
and puts it in front of me on the table.
"Sit down, missy. Have some beans.
Don't know when we last had company.
It's not much, but we share
what it is. *Mi casa, su casa.*"
He laughs, not a real laugh, but one
for everybody to hear.

"Sit down!"
I sit.
Redbud sits to the left of me.
Memaw ladles stringy tomatoes,
white fish, ground meat,
and crawdads into our bowls.
The sergeant major tosses a newspaper
he has been glancing at onto the wood floor.
It hits with what seems like a slam.
"Nothin'," he says. "Now, you would think
there would be a job out there somewhere
for a man like me, now wouldn't you, soldier?"
But Redbud does not answer him,

so with his bowl of gumbo
in one hand the sergeant major shakes a clean cloth
     napkin out
with his other and tucks it under his chin.
Then, using both hands, he lifts the bowl to his mouth
and slurps crawdads, mystery meat,
and white fish down his throat.
He wipes his chin ever so softly
and then neatly pours brown beer into a tall glass.
He sets the bottle down in a wet ring on the table.
Picks up the glass and gulps the beer,
his Adam's apple jumping at each swallow.
I watch him set the glass down,
empty now.
He sets it exactly in the middle of that neat,
     white ring.
It's as if his hands do things softly and neatly
and are separate from the rest of him.
Soft and white and delicate.
I eat everything,
even crawdads,
mudbugs,
they make me prickle.
I stir my gumbo,
I want to slow down,

empty these crawdads on a napkin,
but I do not dare.
I see the sergeant major
butter his roll
softly
then look at me
as if he just knows I'm up to something,
and I am, anyways I'm up
to thinking something.
He calls Redbud to do this
and move that and fetch this and wipe that.
Redbud without speaking
does it all and then before he sits back down
he gives a silent salute.
And I don't know if the sergeant major knows it
or Redbud knows or maybe even Memaw.
But I do, I know
that the sergeant major's eyes are beaming,
his gold-dust eyes are shining on Redbud.
And because I have not been the light of anybody's eyes
    or life
for a very long time
I stand up
and bringing my right hand to my brow
I salute.

The sergant major looks at me,
his smile wide.
I could not have done better.

And as he picks that
newspaper back up,
hiding those eyes behind the want ads,
I bounce back to Redbud's transportation room.
Redbud kicks the bed into service.
"Where to!" I shout over what I imagine
to be the crash of ocean waves.
I picture far-off lands, pirates' galleons
filled with gold and silver coin.
I am a commander of the high sea. I am a lionheart.
"Where to?" I shout again.
"Nottingham" is Redbud's answer,
soft and serious as ever,
a faraway look in his eyes.
I steer the boat
as he charts our course.

I sit on the floor
in front of Pop
watching TV.

It is one of those Sunday mornings
I thought forever lasting.

Pop is still wearing his
black rubber boots
from the garden,
where with the sunflowers and zinnias
he builds his garden art.
Art that if not made
right there in the garden,
Pop says,
would look as out of place as a
weather vane atop a skyscraper.
It feels safe here
with Pop
on the couch and me
on the floor.
The Sunday paper
spread like a quilt around us.

Sis having taken my dark-tanning oil
and gone to her friend Val's
to swim in her heated swimming pool.
"I want to go," I told her before she left.
"No," she said, "just lend me your tanning oil."

It is the good kind
with the island coconut smells.
"Please," I said, holding it out to her,
but not quite handing it over.
"No. It will be just the three of us there."
And that was a lie.
Three girls, yes, but about five
boys, including Eddie,
Marc Gilstein, Matt and Alan Jacobs,
and Stephen Mulhern, probably,
from Sis and Val's theater class.
They will play Marco Polo
till they get chill bumps
then run for corn chips
and marshmallow cream pies that
Mrs. Stead has set out on the patio table
with sodas and . . .
"I want to go," I told Sis again.
"No." And she meant it,
seated in her car,
the '82 blue Honda Civic station wagon,
that could pass for Mr. Magoo's.
"No!"
"But," I said, watching the car roll down the hill,
"you have my dark-tanning oil."

Now it's just Pop and me
watching TV.
Spider-Man and friends
G.I. Joe, Transformers.
And during the commercial I say,
"Bet you seen a lot of action, huh, Pop?"
Action being what the sergeant major
tells of on his mornings with Redbud
and now me, when I get a chance
I go over there hoping
to find out all about him,
this man with the voice like a steam pipe
and the hands like a girl's.
I say again, "Bet you seen a lot of action, huh, Pop?"
"Action?"
"In the conflict," I say.
"Conflict?"
"The war, Pop."
"The war?"
I am mad now,
him there sitting on cloud nine
not even hearing me!
Hey up there!

And I knew the sergeant major
had held 'em off
in the Vietnam Conflict
fightin' to the death
if need be
and here is Pop
figurin' to get us
some refreshment
by jigglin' a waffle from the toaster.
"Pop, in the war. Vietnam?"
"Oh, Vietnam. Couldn't guess what you was saying,"
   Pop says,
picking the waffle out with a fork.
"No, Ceil. Gran needed me at the time.
I was the oldest and only son.
Gramps had died. She needed me.
I was happy to stay and help."
"You never went to war?
Never had Nam adventures, like the sergeant major?
Redbud's pop was in Nam," I tell him, saying
Nam the way the sergeant major says it,
drawing on the "a."
"Had any number of adventures," I say.
"Three tours he did there."
Pop cuts the waffle,

handing me half.

"You don't say. Mighty brave."

"Yes, he was, and he was in the war
and you weren't, huh?"

Which meant that the sergeant major
was brave and Pop was not.

"So what did you do to help Gran?"

"All sorts of odd jobs," he says, sipping his coffee
while I take a bite of waffle.

"Mostly, I read to her."

"You read to her?"

"Yes, Ceil. Your gran liked the sound of my voice.
The way I wrapped it around a book.
Comforting is what she said,
like the hum of a lily pond."

He bites into his waffle,
letting strawberry topping
dribble down onto his pajama shirt.

Newspaper between us like a cement wall.

Not one bit like The Hulk
or G.I. Joe.

More like Dagwood
in the Blondie comics.

Yeah, Dagwood.

What would Dagwood

do in case of danger?
Send in Blondie, what else?

And for some odd reason unknown to me
I want Sis here.
Sis would chuckle,
pat Pop on the top of his head
where his part is
and say just the right thing
to both of us.
Sis is natural in situations
like this.

Like when she brought it up that we
always say goodbye to each other
before leaving the house.
Something about the personal touch missing now that
    Mom is gone
and Sis being responsible for bringing it back.
But not really.
Sis's personal touch is Sis's personal touch.

We never go out without saying goodbye, though.
Goodbyes that are full of meaning.
Because we know that if one of us

does not come back
that certain goodbye
will have to last in our memories
a lifetime.
We make it count.
Always we touch,
a hand, a shoulder, we feel the warmth
when we look in the other's eye
we talk true and from the gut.

We will never leave
without a trace of the other.

So, Sis is natural in situations like this.
I am not.

"I got to go," I say.
I swing the screen door wide.
"Cecelia, be back here by noon," Pop calls out.
"I've got something of a surprise for you."
"Sure thing, Pop," I say,
but already not wanting
the something of a surprise.
On the path
that leads to the road

I twirl and twist
to see if I can get dizzy
the way I used to as a kid.
I find the beat-up chicken wire fence
that lies mostly on the ground.
It rattles
as I teeter-totter
to the front walkway.
The house is mouse quiet.
I am at the beat-up screen door
pounding in the
way of Redbud.

"She won't come," he says.
I look to see the sergeant major
kneeling beside his truck
digging in a red box full of tools.

I move on over there,
tripping on a pine tree root,
tumbling beside him.
He smiles down at me.
My shoe is untied
so natural as nothing
he ties it in a neat little bow

using his carved hands,
like ivory.

His Chevy truck is up on tire ramps in the drive.
The tool box is at my shoulder.
He reaches behind me for a wrench.
I don't say a thing.
He does. "Got this truck at auction.
Paid almost nothing, and guess what?
I got almost nothing!" And he laughs,
a real laugh this time, deep and dimply.
"Want to do something for me?"
"Sure," I say, watching his eyes.
"See there, under the truck?
Oil pan right there in the center.
There's a bolt. Tighten it up, will you?"
"I can't get in there," I tell him.
"Sure you can," he says,
handing me the wrench.
And there is something not only about those eyes
but the way he expects me
to do it all and do it right,
that I do dig my way under the truck
and of course

I feel all out of breath in this tight spot.
I get out of breath
whenever the four sides of me are closed in.
Gates shutting. Walls moving in.
I get a little dizzy, but then I spot the bolt,
and begin to tighten, not the way Pop had told me
but Uncle Troy—because Uncle Troy
cares about his cars—Pop cares less.
I tighten righty tighty–lefty lucy.

I am here this afternoon
for all afternoon
listening to the sergeant major
talk of the old days,
and the good times back then,
and the hopes he has for a job,
any job that will take him away from here.
And he looks at his own house
in a way that maybe he shouldn't.
A way that I've seen only once,
and that was from Mrs. Stark
down at Stark's grocery when
a woman disappeared without
paying for a loaf of bread.

I am watching, too,
the sergeant major work
with his hands,
knowing his tools in the way Pop
knows his paints.
I smell his sweat—
a mix of cologne,
grease and Pall Mall cigarettes.
He is exact about his work.
No mistakes.
Not like Pop.
Pop who is surrounded by flowers
and herbs, soft, sweet smells,
shiny clean,
lost in thought.
Where mistakes are welcome,
expected even.
He has a pile of mistakes
behind the shed.
"Someday," he says,
"that pile will amount to something eventful."
So far it's amounted to spidery weeds,
red dirt, and giant fire ants.

Now, the sergeant major's Chevy truck motor roars
as he has started it up
and he is looking at me.
"Let's take her for a ride!"
he yells to me over the commotion,
and he does not know that I can't.
He is not like other fathers
giving warnings and such.
Throws caution to the wind.
Is that where it belongs after all?

And I want to.
I am practically there with him
in that truck speeding down the dirt road, then on to the
    highway.
His white-toothed smile attracting everybody.
And he would be so proud of the truck and of me!
But of course I remember,
No. No rides with anyone.
"No," I say, and he is gone out of there,
leaving grease rags
and Maggie and me behind
in a puff from the tailpipe
and a quick backwards wave.
He is gone

and wherever he is off to
will be an adventure.
Then I am mad at Pop.
Chin-hard mad.
No cars ever!
How could he know?
And where is he, anyway, where?
To even know how good I am being.

So, natural as nothing
I go there the next day, too.
I spy Maggie first off.
Maggie with the rusty white coat,
floppy, furry ears,
brown eyes, soft and serious,
eyes that remind me of Redbud's.
The sergeant major has just tossed a tennis ball.
Maggie is loping, drooling,
her tail wagging,
but when she sees me
she goes for me
and not the ball.
He turns, his eyes on her,
then a stone nicks her ear
but I have her collar now,

my eyes locked in his
unshining ones.
How does gold dust turn to oil?
His eyes are dark and deep,
lighting a liquid fire on me.
"C'mon along, Maggie," I say,
letting her lick my fingers
till I discover the ball along the fence line
and don't think anymore to find Redbud.
I lead her back to him with it.
"Every dog needs to do a little finger-lickin'," I say,
handing him back the tennis ball.
"Every dog needs discipline," he says,
grabbing hold of Maggie's collar.
"See here," he says, pointing to some dug holes near the
   porch.
"Yes."
"Maggie dug those.
Out here night after night
digging up my yard."
"Uh-huh?" I say.
He is twisting the hose knob,
and then filling one hole after the other.
Then he throws the hose out of reach,
the water still gurgling out the end.

He takes Maggie by the collar,
a choke collar which jangles with one tag,
grabs her big head and shoves her nose
down in the water-filled hole.
I catch my breath with her
and I don't begin to breath again
until he has brought her nose out.
"This'll teach her to dig holes back here," he says,
smiling up at me,
but dragging Maggie on to the next hole.
I see her snuffle. Air bubbles!
She has forgotten to keep her breath in this time.
She digs her back paws into the soft ground.
But he only holds her there longer this time.
"Discipline," he says, "every new thing needs discipline.
This one here should have got it at puppy stage."
Why? and again, why?
But I do not ask it.
My eyes are on Maggie, she sputters,
then he lets her go, watching her run
out of sight, back to her post, probably.
And I am sorry she did not see fit to come back to me.
But then why should she?
I did not help her one bit.

But I am thinking he is not right,
until I look into his eyes and see how serious he's gone.
And why should I doubt him?
When is the last time anybody, anybody
has taken me so seriously,
looked into my eyes so hard,
to talk to me of anything?
"Won't hurt her," he says, "only show her not to."
Why shouldn't I believe him,
discipline is how it is?
But for all my wanting to know
about him, for all my
being curious, I am more afraid
than before and that little something
in my mind that warns me
is now nagging
do not go in there—
because here I am at Redbud's door the very next day.
I promised to meet him today,
and a promise is a promise.
So I peep in,
putting one foot in the house.
"Hello?"
My voice comes back to me off the walls,
I sound older, bigger, braver.

Half in and half out
of the door, I stand.
The crackle of brush
and the buzz of beetles behind me,
the smell of sour kitchen in front of me.
Through the far kitchen window
I make out a hornet's nest
and hornets swimming around it.
"Hello?"
A foot falls.
The door closes.
The sergeant major's eye,
green and gold,
tight, tight smile,
not spilling anything,
not even a howdy.
And the same
ripped T-shirt
on a shoulder that does not
look real.
It could be made out of wax.
"Redbud here?" I squeak.
"Well, if it isn't missy. Come on in.
Come all by yourself, did you?"
"I knocked, but—"

"Never mind that. Come on.

I got something to show you back of the house."

"I came for Redbud," I say.

I do not want to follow.

I could end up in the room that yelped of itself.

"I'll just wait." And somehow these three words

come out as if I mean them.

He looks at me with a crooked grin.

A wink.

I see wasps swimming around his shaved head

as he stands there in front of that far window.

"Okay. I'll bring her to you."

He's gone to the back of the house.

I stand there wondering who "her" is.

And if I should leave now.

He comes back with a cardboard box,

there is scratching inside, whimpering.

He opens it.

The scratching and whimpering don't stop.

I move toward the box,

closer,

then,

inside

in the eyes

of brown

I see a puppy.
It lifts its tiny eyes
to see me.
Tiny brown eyes
that look out of
a dusty coat of fur.
It moves then
to get out of the box,
and there is something else,
a growl almost.
The sergeant major slaps it twice
on the nose.
He shuts the puppy back up.
"Needs discipline," he says.
I step back.
"Every new thing needs discipline."
He sets the box on the table.
The puppy is quiet.
The sergeant major lifts a tall water glass,
puts it to the light of the window.
It isn't beer this time,
but maybe tea.
Why? I say to myself,
and then I say it out loud, "Why?"
He turns at me.

I think against me.

"To survive," he says.

He looks at me with those green-gold eyes,

shining, those black pupils look right through me.

I am frightened.

I cannot move,

and like that puppy

I am whimpering inside,

and like that hypnotized snake

I am charmed, too.

"Suppose," he says,

"you're put in a pickle.

Enemy to the left of you.

Enemy to the right.

The mind begins to think," he says.

"No way out! One of the scariest things you will ever
    know."

And then he is in front of me, looking at me,

down into my eyes.

I look to his waspy head,

strong arms,

and remember the door is closed, bolted shut.

"Ah, but that's when the training comes in," he says.

"The discipline.

You remember you got your forty-five on your hip.
You draw the old friend out and let loose."
I see his hand
come up
then,
"Bang! bang! bang!"

I am not dead.
It is his joke.
He stands there pointing his finger.
He laughs.
I laugh, too.
Sure, I'm glad
to be out of that hard place.
And isn't it kind of funny?
I want to believe him.
I want to believe discipline is the way it is.
Discipline is what it takes to make a person brave.
And now he says, "It's Maggie's pup. I'll learn this one
    right.
Discipline, missy. Don't you forget it."
He turns. "Soldier left early this morning.
Haven't seem him since.
When you meet up, tell him to be home early.

There's hogs to slaughter."
I look at him to see if he is serious.
He winks. His green-gold dancing eyes.
I laugh again and I am out the door on shaky legs,
like I'd been kneeling in church for a half hour.
I jump to get them to set down right on the path.
Then I know I am on the road.
Discipline.
I jump again,
coming down hard
to the cement.

I see footprints in the sandy dirt.
Small and pigeon-toed
footprints.
Redbud.
I tell him as quick as I catch up,
"There's hogs to slaughter.
Don't want to miss that, do we, soldier?"
I am laughing.
He looks at me.
He sees my whole self in that look.
I am afraid he knows then how scared I am,
and he will laugh and think,

awww, she's only a girl.
But he squints into the sun and says,
"I'll be there. Not to worry."

We step up our play then.
I want to play war
now that my courage is back.
I want to feel what it's like to be this kind of brave.
A disciplined kind of brave,
with soldiers and guns.
G.I. Joe.

"Not how it is in the movies, Scout," Redbud says.
"My daddy gave mouth-to-mouth to someone shot in
    the face.
People got burned over there and lots died."

And I know how that is.
I know how it is to watch
another loved one die
as you watch that piece of yourself go.
And does the hurt ever go away, really?

"And that is why," he says, "the salute is so important.
It's what is left. It's that important."

And then what I hear is the woods,
the redheaded woodpecker,
the crackle of sweet-smelling pine.
I see spots of sunlight,
and the silver pools of leaves.
The still pool,
black butterflies,
flowers the color of
cold plums.
All of it open to us.
Where was my head?
"Okay," I say.
"Let's play Merlin the Magician."
Another Saturday cartoon we watch,
not G.I. Joe or Transformers,
but about Merlin in his tower
over the English sea
with his little-bitty bird.

"Redbud," I say, "You be my little-bitty bird."
"No bitty bird," he says.
"Yes you are. You act like one.
Doing all that stuff
when your daddy says, 'Do this! Do that!

Hop to it, soldier!'
My bitty bird," I say it again soft and teasing.
I scruff his head.
He moves away.
"You don't know how it is."
"Then how is it? Tell me."
"Scary. It's scary at home."
"Too scary for a bitty bird?" I say softly.
"Yeah" is all he tells me.
And again I want to make it all right for this kid.

The way I did for my mother.
Brushed her hair off her forehead
when she no longer could. One time
some of that hair fell onto my arm.
I flicked it off like flecks of cold snow,
and thought of my very first doll.
Her hair as white as snow
and how when I combed the bangs some of that
steely hair came out in my lap.
It's not supposed to happen to mothers.
They are not dolls. I am
not supposed to be taking
care of her. I am not
supposed to be dipping

my fingers in ice water
to let her suck on them.
Not supposed to be wiping coffee from her chin.
Not supposed to be breathing
for her, breathing—take my
breath—and then another
to live another day.
To see her look at me
once more and
please, smile, that long crooked smile.

When your mother is dying
you get used to holding
her tears,
her pain.
And when she's gone,
so's you don't feel your own pain,
your own hurt,
you look for something to hold again.
I looked and found Redbud.

"I am Merlin," I tell him.
"And I need a wand."
With a bow and a cough
I lift a gnarly knobby stick

and like an old man bucking at the rain
I bully everything in sight.
When that doesn't work,
I twirl and bow and giggle
and forget.
Waving the wand
and highstepping
on and off the path, I sing out,
"I'll make the stars tumble from the sky
the moon rise above the water
and children turn inside out,
inside out, inside out
shellfish, tadpoles,
timber bugs, drool,
an ocean,
laughter,
go lively,
no school!"

Redbud marches
behind me
as I twirl the wand,
touching everything.
And it seems
just then

we are magic,
and the woods are alive
with every bee,
dragonfly, insect, bird, and animal.
It is a way of being lighter.
Not more than we are.
A magic that weaves its spell
until I believe
I have made the wild plum tree blossom,
the dragonflies shimmer blue,
and the hawk circle to the circling of my
wand, and Redbud finally fall asleep
in the grass.
I kneel down with him
close to his breath.
His brow is not knitted so tight.
He has a light coat of
sweat and smells of honeysuckle and wild rose.
I sit beside him and wind my stick in the dirt
the way I would if I were warming
a stick for a fire.
I lay my head on Redbud's stomach,
and before I fall off to sleep
I hear him ever so softly say,
"Scout, this is my real home."

It is a country nap.
Half hour at most.
We wake and rub our eyes, then start where we left off.
Me crowning him king.
Him placing me in the Tower of London.
"No. No," I say. "Not my fingers!"
Because I'd read in some dilly of a book
at May's house how King Henry VIII
had Anne Boleyn's pinky chopped off.
Redbud spares me this.
I go to the tower, though,
where from a low
branch of a mesquite tree
I spy the back of a coyote not twenty feet away.
It turns.
Its eyes
yellow like a cat,
clever and bold.
Does it know
I am here watching?
Yes.
And it knows that Redbud is on the ground
not ten feet from where it is stopped.

This coyote fears nothing.
Not shotgun.
Starvation.
Starvation?
Is it hungry?
Will it attack?
Redbud?
Its dark coat,
cold eyes,
not green gold
not shiny like wax and tight,
not hard,
but soft,
nimble,
light,
wild.
Kind?

It trots off without looking back.
I don't tell Redbud
he was this close to dying
because I don't believe it.
He is closer to being dead
at home with the sergeant major.

Then I say so long,
too soon I say it.
Redbud still wants to play.
But I am tired.
All this thinking on things.
All this wondering what brave is.
I am all mixed up inside.
I am halfway home when it hits me,
Pop has a surprise!

But Aldo is here.
He and Uncle Troy
have dropped by for dinner,
which they do sometimes
when Auntie Lidia is still working.
But dinner isn't for another hour.
Pop and Uncle Troy are watching TV.
Aldo's head is on Uncle Troy's lap.
He looks up from a sleep.
A bat!
He has a bat costume on!
Oh, no, what a goof!
"Cecelia, we're having turnips tonight for dinner," he says,
not fully awake yet,

and that is how I know he has been waiting to tell me
  this.
He has committed it to memory.
"I told Dad, Cecelia won't like turnips so don't bring
  them,
but seeing as how my mom does and she's coming later
we're having turnips. So there."
"Hey, Aldo," I say, not wanting to talk
here with Uncle Troy and Pop looking on,
"want to play Yahtzee in my room?"
He looks at me like he does not want to leave Uncle
  Troy,
but at the same time does not want to miss out
on a chance to play in my room.
Then he flies at me, snapping his bat wings.
We play Yahtzee five minutes in my room before
he can no longer keep it to himself.
"I am going to be a bat. What about you?"
Even though Halloween isn't for six months.
"A witch."
"Every year you're a witch.
What's so fun about that?"
"Witches stew bats," I say, without even cracking a
  smile.
And I am buzzing with joy! Ha ha, I got you, Aldo!

He spreads his netted wings
and pretends to fly around my room.
When he jumps on my bed I jump on him.
"Get off!" I yell.
"Get off!" he yells.
We roll to the floor.
I sit on one of his wings.
He stands up and flaps one wing.
"Look what you did!"
It is broken in half.
Like a kite that's been pitched in the dirt.
That's not ever going up again.
"Sorry. But why did you jump on my bed?"
He doesn't answer. Just flaps around like an injured bat.
"Let's ask the eight ball!" Aldo shouts.
He is all wound up,
looking in drawers on dresser tops for my Magic 8 Ball.
It gives answers to questions put to it.
Like yes, or no, or maybe.
Aldo is digging in my underwear drawer, my closet.
"I found it! Here, here," he says, jumping at me.
"Shhh, will you?" I say. "You want our dads to come
    up?"
"Let's play eight ball!"

He sits there giving me the injured bat plea.
Kind of like the Jack Russell terrier smile.
So natural as nothing I fall for it.
"All right. One question.
That's all we get to ask."
We sit in the center of my sleeping bag.
Aldo on one pillow.
Me on the other.
"You ask it," I say.
He looks at me like a bat,
with the black puppy nose,
and pointy ears.
And he knows just what to ask,
just what I am thinking, right now.
And isn't that how these games go?
You thinking of it the same time
as your best buddy and then,
whaddya know, the game gives you the same answer.
People say it's voodoo.
I say it's the odds.

"Will Cecelia eat turnips tonight?" is what Aldo asks.
We tip the ball back and forth
and wait for the answer to settle
in the slurpy bubbles.

He looks. "Yes! It says yes. Look. See for yourself."
I don't want to look. Not because of what it says,
but because he is shoving it in my face.
"Cecelia fraidy cat," he says. "Look.
Cecelia chicken. Look. It is a yes!"
I take it from him then and look,
then I drop it on his slipper-sock foot.
Aldo chases me out to the hall.
I skid round the corner and into Pop's room,
slamming the door.
"I'll get you," he says. "You just wait."

I sit on Pop's bed waiting for Aldo to get tired
of hanging outside the door.
I lie back on Pop's giant pillow.
My mother's white satin one beside me
with the red heart in the middle,
and the embroidered word in pink, LOVE.
I know Pop does not sleep with it,
but moves it from dresser to bed,
bed to dresser,
morning and night.

Straight ahead on the wall is a picture
of three children kneeling beside a bed.

Two of them boys, one a girl.
One of the boys could have been Redbud,
same blond hair,
brown eyes, smile.
But of course it isn't.
This is a long-ago painting.
Funny but I never knew it was in here.

"Cecelia, your pop wants you pronto,"
comes Aldo's voice from the other side of the door.
Didn't he ever get tired of trying to trick me?
"Tell him to go count pineapples in Honolulu.
I'm not coming out."
I hear Aldo race down the hall.
His slippered feet like buckshot on the stairs, ping, ping,
    ping.
I shoot out of the room after him,
down the stairs and into the kitchen.
"I never wanted to say it, Pop. It was Aldo who
    made me."
Aldo stands there pointing at me,
an awful grin on his bat face. "She did too."
"Just never mind that," Pop says, turning back to mash-
    ing the potatoes on the stove.
"More important things to do than chase you wild ones."

But I am thinking, mashed potatoes are more important
    than me?

I eat the turnips with a pork chop
and later talk my uncle into
giving us a ride in his Trans Am.

When we get back,
mine and Uncle Troy's hair is plastered to our necks.
I am cold.
And I can't explain it,
because the air is warm
out in the night
the stars high and bright
But I am chilled
and coughing.
I run upstairs to get my sweater but
spy Sis's friend Val,
who is in the bathroom staring into the mirror.
She is the thin one.
Thin man,
is what Sis calls her.
She is nice, though,
and has a kind smile.
She turns it toward me now.

I see that Sis's bedroom door is open.
She is getting ready for a sleepover.
Val is here so maybe Jillie will come and Wanda Sue.
I don't miss any of this.
And I probably won't have sleepovers when I am sixteen.
I will have people over in the day
to make music in the sun.
For sure I am going to learn to play the bass clarinet
when I get to high school.
I missed all that this year,
the first year of band,
because, well,
because I am not ready to make music yet.

Sis's room.
Like Disney World in the commercials.
Her canopy bed a tented castle
of pink and blue sheers.
Gold ribbons, like castle-top banners,
pinned, float on the air from the ceiling fan.
Draperies shield her huge closet
like the skirt of Cinderella's gown,
gold-sequined, white see-through sheers,
border a sweet-pea green velvet cloth.

All bought downtown on Main Street,
from Millie's Remnants & Pieces shop.
Bought at Millie's but
made lovely by Sis, who bargain hunts,
but comes away smiling with silver-thread cloth,
bows for the cost of a dime,
buttons at a penny apiece.

Gold buttons, green buttons,
turquoise and yellow,
trailing in Sis's room like coins.

And she even has this cool pink plastic material
that she has used for curtains
that sparkle in the sun
and kind of glow when it rains.
And in here are three full-length mirrors Pop
purchased at Wal-Mart but not inexpensive ones,
tall ones, wide and nice.
Sis has placed fringed cushions
to the sides for people
(mainly me) to sit and admire
the person fashioning herself in the mirror (usually Sis),
but sometimes, just sometimes,
it's me,

in a gold tiara and black velvet robe,
gold cord at my waist,
white slippers,
and bold-colored scarf, the size of a flag,
my hair swinging at my shoulders
as I flounce about.
Sometimes it's me.
The solid one. I am more solid
than Sis and I will be shorter, they tell me.
My hands are long but not delicate.
I will play the bass clarinet easily,
my right pinky finger reaching to the lowest key.

And somebody says, everybody says,
including Sis,
my pudgy stomach will
flatten by itself.
The way Sis explained it,
I will wake up and that pudge will
be in all the right places.

And when I flounce in front of the mirrors
it's as though I already know this.
And twirling
in the black velvet robe and colored scarf,

I feel it.
Like rose petals,
I am dewy, and fresh, and smell boldly beautiful.

It is as I bow, my tiara slipping,
Pepe right there to fetch it,
that I look up into the mirror
and see myself as a young queen,
like the medieval queen on the card my mother
gave to me.
I catch my breath because,
like on the card, above my head
are not the gargoyle gods,
but two skeleton heads,
the sockets of which
look to me, but, of course do not see.
Their mouths gaping holes.
Then, in an instant, I know it is just that Sis has forgotten
to take these two cardboard skeletons down from last
    year's Halloween party.

The shiver I felt gone now and
replaced by Pop
come in from outside,
downstairs with Sis.

Their voices rise up to me
like muffin batter baking,
delightful and welcome.

I place the tiara on the dresser top
where I got it from,
the robes back under the bed,
the slippers I forget to take off.
And when I run to the kitchen
I feel the soles soft on the kitchen tile
but it's too late.
She already sees them,
her slippers.
"Where?" she starts at me,
before Pop glides in front of her
and offers her this week's crossword.
She stops in midwalk,
takes it from him, smiles at his smile.
And then they are on the topic of fruit.

Oh yeah! Pepe and
I hop the steps two by two
like the lucky ducks we are.
The slippers I place back in the dark closet
for another time.

Aldo sleeps over that same night.
He sleeps in the spare room.
He goes into the hall bathroom
stays in there for a long time
leaving a sticky hair spray smell in the hall.
I swear it's even leaked out the doorjambs,
and is hair-spray-sticky on the hall carpet.
When he does come out
he is wearing his race-car pajamas.
His hair combed into a black helmet.
One of those bike helmets,
but only with a fin in the back.
He smells of toothpaste.

"I am going out back," I tell him.
I curl next to Pepe on the back porch
in my sleeping bag and watch the stars
that are bright in the night sky,
reminding me of soap suds
winking in dishwater.
I hear Pop starting the washing machine
in the laundry room off the porch.
I hear Sis's music coming from her room

and wonder is she up there dancing with Val and
     Wanda Sue?
I connect the stars like dots.
Finding the Big Dipper,
the star in Orion's belt,
and by now Pepe is snoring.
I am about to sleep, too, when I hear
a scuttle and leaves move.
And then I see Redbud running out of the bushes,
     calling,
"I've run away."
And I am up,
and saying what it is I knew I would say,
what I hoped I could say when it came to this,
"Stay here!"

And he does
and I drag out the extra sleeping bag
from the hall closet
without anybody noticing,
and microwave popcorn,
and a comic book.
And it is as I am reading Spider-Man to him,
(and him just getting out of a jam,

and Redbud not caring a twit
but sleeping like a good puppy),
that Aldo flashlights us.
The beam of light blinding.
"Turn that thing off, will you! He's sleeping."
How cold he gets on these hot nights.
All wrapped up in blankets
like my mother in her last days.
No warming her up.
Her eyes grew cold.
That was the worst.
No me in them,
no Ceil, no Pop, no Sis.
Really we were gone before she actually left.
Is that death?
You dying with the other person?
You dying with your mother?
Your family dying?

Aldo is talking to me. "What did you say, Cecelia?
Who *is* he? Is that Redbud?"
But I am not going to explain Redbud to him.
And I am not going to pretend to Redbud that Aldo
is cute and friendly.

Aldo can be all that,
but there is just no telling when his tricks will come.
And in a flash, a thought,
I have for the first time anticipated Aldo's tricks.
Maybe, I am not falling quite so easily.
Maybe I have covered that gaping hole with gauze.
I sit there staring into the dark.
"Oh heck, I'm going inside. I am no fly bait,"
　　Aldo says,
trailing his flashlight like a long skirt behind him.

Mayflies big as bumblebees buzz around us.
I cover Redbud up with the front of the sleeping bag,
listening to him sniffle and cough,
always a part of him,
just as it came to be a part of my mother.
His runny nose,
the familiar smell of sickness.
And I look at the sky, at Orion's belt again,
pointing it out to him
already asleep.
And it feels so lonely and I can't hear
Pop or Aldo
only the turn of the washing machine.

Only I told him
before he nodded off.
I told him about my dream.
The one about the mirror
one of those ones
like we have in our bathroom
that when you open it up
on the other side are Band-Aids and aspirin and stuff.
In my dream, though, the mirror opens up
and you know what is on the other side? You!

In the kitchen the next morning
Aldo comes in rubbing his eyes.
The tops of his Spider-Man underwear peeking out
from his pajama bottoms.
"Sit down, Aldo," Pop says,
sliding waffles off the griddle and onto Aldo's plate.
Aldo slides in beside Auntie Lidia,
(who has come by before going to work
just so she can be with Aldo before
he begins his morning with us).
Auntie Lidia stacks three ham slices in front of him,
then pours him a glass of milk.
Aldo is all Auntie Lidia sees.

"Because," Pop says, "she has no free time for the boy's
      sports games, or to help him with his homework,
or to even cook him a decent meal.
What with her working like a slave
all day long down at McCleary's Drug Store."

I slip on my slippers from under the table,
signal for Pepe and am out the back door too quick
for even anybody to free their mouths of waffle and ham.

I am padding around in my bunny-ear slippers
beside him.
Him asleep. So sound.
Not a bounce in him.
The two of us like this on my back porch.
I drink grape Kool-Aid.
A glass for him at my elbow.
And nothing else.
I know Redbud doesn't want ham
and does not care for Pop's waffles,
which are thick and dimply,
and I don't have a chocolate cake.

Pepe with the morning jitters
jumps and paws at me.

Next, he's off chasing a squirrel.
The sun about froze off all the dark.
Soon it'd be on us,
hot as tomato soup.
How I wish he'd wake up.

And then he does,
and of course we go fishing.
I do not want or need to tell Pop
about Redbud running away.
Pop is too busy, busy mixing up waffle batter,
serving ham and juice and milk,
to listen about Redbud,
to hear what it is I might have to say,
that maybe I have thought about it,
thought that I am getting in too deep.
Deep into matters I do not, or should not be into at all.

So I grab my fish pole,
and Sis's brand new one,
because she will never use it.
She would not be caught
dead casting a line into the local waters.
"I might come away with a fish," she has told me.
"I would come away with a fish. Yeck!"

Redbud and I cast bologna to the fish,
lie back on our elbows,
and wish the sun behind a cloud.
I am jumpity as a grasshopper,
sucking a piece of grass,
kicking up dirt,
twisting a piece of my hair
while rocking back and forth,
swaying my hips to the music
in my head,
Rock around the clock tonight.

"Can't you never stay still?" he asks.
"How am I s'posed to catch fish
with you like spit on a hot griddle?"

I can't help it.
I can't tell him why I am so antsy.
It's like I got hold of Mexican jumping beans
and swallowed them.
It's like I get before I come down with the flu,
and have to stay in all day.
Or like I got before
Gran called from Ohio
to tell us Grandpapa had had a stroke

and was in the hospital.
By the time she called
I was already grounded in my room.
My being antsy had played itself out in the backyard,
where I'd picked up a shovel and started digging.
Didn't stop till Pop spied me from the kitchen window.
At which time I was headed to China lickety-split.

But we aren't catching anything,
and I'll just bet it's the bait.
Yesterday's worms.
And then I remember Pop.
He always stocks my bait
in the refrigerator
and I just wonder about that surprise he has for me.
When I tell Redbud,
he gets this funny look on his face,
then says, "You go, Scout.
I am going on back home."
I run all the way home
not thinking about why it is he ran away.
Not thinking about the sergeant major,
Maggie, Memaw, any of it.
And the Trans Am is not in the drive,
and that means the Troys are gone.

The Troys is what Pop calls my uncle and his family.
It's like Uncle Troy owns his family same as his
    Trans Am.
But unlike his Trans Am that he can polish till it gleams,
he tries and tries with Auntie Lidia and Aldo
but somehow they resist all that spiffing-up.

In the parlor I am
all out of breath.
Sis is there on the couch reading.
"Aldo left you something over there," she says,
without looking up from her book.
It is a note with his scrawl, "Cecelia, who *are* you?"
Grabbing a pencil, I write on the same paper.
I am Night. So try to find me, why don't you?
I stuff it in the cookie jar,
hoping that when he is dreaming of chocolate chips
and sticks his hand in the jar,
he comes away with my question,
try to find me, why don't you?
"Cecelia," Sis says, "the next time you leave
a poem for Eddie, sign your own name, please."
And I know the poem she is talking about.
The one about the frizzy head
and kiss on the mouth.

The poem I left on the TV
as I danced to a jitterbug tune.
And I blame it on the jitterbug.
"I had a tune in my head.
A dance in my step.
And it just spilled out onto the paper,"
I tell her.

She doesn't care.
"Eddie thought it was cute," she says.
And I'll just bet she got a kiss on the mouth.

I find Pop at the sink
in his apron doing dishes,
singing too loud to the radio.
Sis's plastic cups, soda bottles,
popped balloons
from her sleepover
peppered all over the counter.
I think of the sergeant major,
the way he keeps careful
watch on Memaw as she clears
the plates from the table
and how before she
brings them to the sink

she stops and waits till he gives her leave.
How everything is neat as a pin.
No confetti in the hair or on the eyelashes,
or dark liquids left in soda bottles,
or counters covered in trash!
I shake the thought
of how silly Pop looks
right out of my head.
"What is it, Pop, my surprise?"
He sets down the dishrag,
steps to the refrigerator,
reaches in and pulls out
a carton.
"Guaranteed," he says.
A piece of yellow confetti falls
from his dark hair.
"Guaranteed?"
"These are special chicken livers," he adds,
"from Joe Cool's Bait Shop.
For you and your friend, Buddy Red."
That's the name Redbud goes by with Pop, Buddy Red.
'Cause one day when we went for the lemonade,
I says, "Pop, this is Buddy,"
and Redbud he says, "Red,"
and all Pop got was, Buddy Red.

Pop hands me the carton.
"Sure, Pop, we'll go.
But no little fish this trip.
I'll bring you back
a catfish big as a seal."

"I was thinking," Pop says,
"we could have a catfish fry come Sunday.
Corn on the cob, hush puppies.
Invite Auntie Kate, Uncle Samuel from Grapevine, the
    neighbors."
"Why?" I ask. "Why have a party now,
with Easter vacation almost over and school starting
    up?"
"Well," Pop says, "the school's not going anywhere
and most folks are back at work.
Hanley's has picked them up again
after that layoff.
If you ask me that's when we need to have a party.
Right in the middle of all that responsibility.
Remind people of what life is all about."
"Fun?"
"You bet!"

And that's how Pop used to be
before my mother died,
watching even a worm
nudge its way home.
He was that close to everything.
Everyone. Miss Nethers,
who hardly ever cleans her house.
He brought her fried chicken on Sundays.
And Joe Girardi, who can't hear a speck,
he brought him the Sunday morning newspaper.
"He can read, can't he?"
is what Pop told me when I asked him why he did that.

Now Pop is going on about the party.
"What'd you say?"
and I've got hope again
like before and before that,
so I stop that hoping but say,
"Sure, a big day."

"Yeah, a big day. Spark things up.
I'll bake that strawberry cake you like
with the cream-cheese icing.
It'll be a big time.
You go down to the river and bring back a giant catfish."

"As big as a seal is more like it," I say.
"That's the kind, catfish as big as a seal."

Pop grabs plates out of the cupboard,
slides a pie from the oven.
"How about a piece of cherry pie?"
We didn't always start at the top of the menu.
Pop slices, humming.
Something is scratching at the screen door.
I slide from my seat,
crack the door open to see
it is Pepe.
He pinches his nose in the crack
just like some slippery trout.
His whole self in the space
of a cracker box.
He jumps into the kitchen,
then licks all my cherry filling
off my plate.
The way he'd slipped in the house
the way he brushed past me
the way he takes my pie
I slap his nose hard, twice.
"Down, Pepe! Down!"
My plate slips to the floor,

crashes and splinters into little red pieces.

Pepe slinks back.

I shout loud and angry.

"Out, Pepe! Get out that door!"

Pepe slips through the door

before I kick it shut on his behind.

Pop does not look at me.

I sit up on the stool

licking my cherry fingers.

"Another piece?" Pop asks.

"Sure," I say.

Pop slices the pie slowly, saying,

"I don't remember you ever being that way with Pepe."

"Well, Pepe needs discipline, Pop."

"Discipline is how it is? That slap on his nose like that?"

I turn my attention to pie.

Something like discipline you don't discuss. You just do.

That's how it is with the sergeant major anyhow.

"Supposin'," I say,

"Pepe was between a rock and a hard place.

Coyotes to one side, wild pig to the other.

Why, without discipline, he wouldn't survive.

Old Pepe'd be a goner."

"You suppose so?" Pop says.

"I do."

"Now supposin', just supposin'," Pop says,
"ol' Pepe in that place between the rock and that other.
Now suppose that coyote he acts all sly and wily,
and those wild pigs, they're all mouthy and hungry like
    they get,
and poor little Pepe there looking out
and knows sure as Swiss cheese there's a way out,
he knows, if he can just find it
before those mongrels close in on him.
He knows it sure enough, except he can't smell a thing
'cause his nose been done slapped to cauliflower.
Now suppose that!"
Pop collects the dishes with some noise, sends me off.
Only interest he takes in me
and it's to yell at me!
Yell, yell, yell!
I yell it back,
only outside now
on the path.
A yell he can't hear is best.

find Redbud on the path.
I am walking behind him
and watching his rucksack
bobbing on his belt.
Watching it bobbing
up and down
up and down
back and forth.
His little figure ahead.
Same T-shirt and shorts
and black high-top sneakers,
shoelaces dragging,
walking soft and lively.
His tan shorts hiked up at his belly button
and tied with that cord.
Cough as little as ever.
His neck sunburnt.
Scratches on his leg.
A bruise?

I am truly tired of his wounds.
There isn't one thing I can do.

I think of his father
the sergeant major—
and me all mixed up
like I never was before
and finally I remember Pop is mad at me.
And I am feeling mean,
so mean.
I think of hooking
that rucksack,
reeling it in,
rucksack, chicken livers,
Redbud and all.
Serve him right
for introducing me
to his home, anyhow.
Weren't we all right before?
My family was getting on just fine, before.

We meet a spot
where the river runs slow,
narrow and deep.
The ground is soft,

the grass lazy, high, cozy.
Baiting our hooks, we cast out,
then sit,
then wait.

We watch slow-moving water,
the gnats on top,
gnats at my neck,
at my mouth.
Redbud splashes river water on me
hoping it'll help cut the gnats.
I find a plastic cup and fill it full,
turn it upside down on his head
hoping he will know it didn't.
We watch the bobbers nod
from red to white,
white to red.
He whistles.
I squish ants between my fingers.
He sighs.
I chuckle.
Not a nibble.
All afternoon
I dream
of snow white meat

smoking on the
side-yard grill.
The party.
Not a nibble.

Guaranteed, my patootie.
Guaranteed to scare 'em off is what.
Pop is wrong.
Some surprise.
I pop the plastic lid back on the carton,
clean the bait off my hook,
fasten the hook to the catch,
set my fishpole aside,
then watch Redbud.
"Just a little longer," he says.
"Cats take their sweet time, you know it."
"I don't know it," I say. "I'm goin'. You comin'?"
"Just a little longer," he says.
He reels in.
Searches the ground for leftover bait.
"Okay, you stay. I'm going," I say.
I pile my tackle box,
chicken livers, knife,
one atop the other,
then with my chin for balance,

bend down and grab my fishpole.
It's when I look up
I see him bait the hook,
then cast
long
to the center
of the river.
I see
the line move with the river.
I see
it go tight
as it hits the current,
and then
it disappears with
the load of a big fish.

Redbud feels all this
before I see it.
His casting arm
straight out,
he reels in,
breathing with it.
The fish tugs,
goes deeper
the way they do.

Redbud moves it
struggling but steady
with the rhythm of the river,
steady to the shore.
I see the flash of white belly
as it comes up.
It is a cat.
A big one.
How proud Pop will be
when I drag that fish on home.
But I know the line,
a six-pound test
will not hold it.
I see Redbud reel
it in fast now,
see his eyes, his jaw
go open as the dead line
blows in the breeze.
Our hope,
our sweet meat
is running with the line.
I still have the hold of the river on me,
the rhythm of the river,
the rhythm of fishing,
the same river current,

same cast,
same slow moves
of Redbud's.
It is all right, I think.
So what? The fish got away.
But then somthing else
not like the rhythm
not like it at all.
Something cold and hard
and blaming.
If he'd had more discipline
that fish would not have got away.
Discipline.
I feel my face burn.
"Why couldn't you have reeled it in slower?
Just like you to do it so fast.
How many times I got to tell you.
Take it easy!"
I tramp, stamp along the highway with him behind me.
The one that leads to the nature center road
that I know I am not supposed to be on.
I am thinking, the one chance I had to make Pop
really happy with me again,
and then I knew I had hoped again.

Cars cut past fast.
I feel the wind they stir up,
and the stinging dirt around my ankles.
The ground bounces with traffic.
A hardness in my heart.
My stomach aches, my head aches.
"No party all on account of you," I mutter.

And Redbud darts off the curb.
I see him out of the corner of my eye,
picking a flower, then another.
and I am really angry,
because I know he is going for those
flowers across the highway,
and cars are going too fast.
"You fool!"
I am crazy angry,
feeling the dirt
spray my ankles,
as a car whizzes past.
I sputter, "Get back over here!"
I don't hear the rhythm of the wood,
the rhythm of the river,
or feel the lightness between us.
I am not thinking,

not listening.

I have a hurt in me.

What is it?

It is hard fear like a ball of wire uncoiled.

"You hear me, stupid!"

He holds these lovely flowers and has this look

sad and happy at the same time.

And I think he is coming toward me,

'cause I yelled at him so.

It is as I turn to go

that I hear the hard

screech of tires,

the squeal,

a yelp—

like a puppy's been hit.

A thud, like he has been knocked down.

The flowers spill as I turn

red ones, blue ones

green stems,

fly

like a flag,

then float to

the street.

The streak of a still-moving red car,

and Redbud

in the gutter,
looking like a rag doll.

I am there.
I touch his hand,
hold his head up and
see blood pool in his ear.
I hear my own blood,
my own heartbeat,
thump thump
and the
rhythm is there
and I hold him close
hold him so close,
so close he will breathe into me
thump thump

I am crying,
screeching,
where is his heartbeat?
I yell at that car,
that teenager driving,
that teenager leaving him like this,
what kind of people
are they to leave

a kid like a rag doll in the road?
I yell for Maggie,
and for her pup,
those snakes,
and frogs.
The deadness of it all.
Mama!

And I am screeching like this
when they find me.
A couple in a station wagon
taking their two kids to soccer practice,
not expecting a sight like this,
not expecting their kids
in the black and tan shorts,
the white V-necked jerseys
would come upon and see
a dying nobody's-child.
Redbud is put into an ambulance.
I am brought back home
after people question me,
so many questions about
what I don't know.
I don't know!
I shake my head, not wanting to talk,

not able to talk.
How does a girl talk after that?
What words can say now
I have no idea.
What can I tell anybody now?
No, only the shake of my head,
only the kick of my foot,
only my shaking body can
tell you how it is.
Can't they know that?
Pop puts me to bed
in my flannels,
even though it is hot.
I shiver, my lip jumps,
teeth rattle, rattle.
Pop pours hot soup in a mug,
tries to get it between
these teeth of mine
that scrape—

Nooo!

Pop sits there and sits there.
He says he will sit until I cry.
A sad, sad bear beside me.

He has not even shaved today.
His flannel shirt is soft and worn.
And I want to hug him all the more,
but something inside me will not give.
I will not hope again.

Well, you will just have to sit there.
And I think I am saying this out loud,
but I see by the way he looks
at me that I am not.
My lips don't even move
with the thought
of what I want to say.
No movement. No sound.
And I like it.
It feels safe
being frozen silent.

So Pop was right,
that stuff about
a nose slapped to cauliflower.
He meant a nose slapped to cauliflower
didn't always know which way to turn.
And wasn't it him who said
at last season's baseball game

when we were all huddled under that
outbuilding, that a body'd be obliged to take cover
in a lightning storm. If he was smart.
But a body unsure of itself
didn't always take cover in a storm.
A body like that was likely
to get struck.
Like that charmed snake.
Hypnotized,
then shot.
And Maggie's puppy
cowering the way it did
when all I wanted was to pet it.
It didn't know a pet from a slap.
The sergeant major's slap slap.
And Redbud,
not knowing
which side of the road
was safe anymore.
I'd confused him
with my badgering,
and how much badgering
he must have taken
from the sergeant major,
slap slap.

Discipline didn't mean a thing.
Just another word for fear.
Another word to hide behind.
It's all clearer now,
the sun coming in my window,
the sharp sounds that crackle the air,
the flap of a loose shingle
on the roof,
kids kicking a ball outside,
radio sounds coming up from downstairs.
My sister in the next bedroom
the little pats
she gives her cheeks
waking up her face mornings.
The spot on my far wall
like a horsetail
swishing a fly.
The ridges of green paint
tiny specks of white.
So clear.
My breathing.
My breathing that I had
not even noticed before.
When you don't talk
you notice all kinds of things.

My Unforgettable Place

I have an unforgettable place.
The place is a lake that you walk around.
It is called the Town Lake.
The Town Lake has fairs and places to climb.
I believe that it is four miles halfway around the
  lake.
When you are on the trail you can see beautiful
  trees.
There is bamboo. It is like a hiding place.
It is a place where up close on your belly you see
  turtles,
big and small.
In this place you can catch crawfish and tadpoles.
The water is greenish, but pretty.
That is my unforgettable place.

By Cecelia Terwiliger

My place in my room
is like that unforgettable place.
I tunnel under my sleeping bag
with comic books and my journal,

my flashlight handy
and peppermints, too.
But not Pepe, not today.
Today I will write.

My hand feels like stone lifted from the grave
of my dead mother.
I don't know, but it writes
as I sit here in my corner of my room,
on and on it writes,
feeling a little lighter
with each word that gets inked
across the page,
feeling a little better, my head
just having written it,
having read it.
I can sit up now,
my back almost straight,
till I am standing,
breathing,
and my poem
is like my breathing,
in out
in out.
Could Redbud's accident or my mom's death stop that?

My breath?
My poem?
Keep it.
Could it?

Redbud would live.
He is in the hospital
in intensive care.
His heart was beating
when they got to him.
His head was hit.
There is some swelling.
The doctors not sure how long
he'd be there,
or what else was affected.
Some scrapes on his elbows and knees,
as if he'd been roughhousing in the front yard,
catching a football maybe, making a pass,
not being thrown.
Can't walk.
Tube fed.
He is alive.
How would it have been
if he were not?

I did not keep him safe behind me.
I did not watch out for him
or keep him close by.
I did not listen like a scout,
or watch like a scout.
If I had, could it have been different?

Pop is doing all he can
at the hospital.
He comes home saying,
"They will make an exception
and let you see him."

Stepping inside the hospital doors
I see all eyes on me.
I feel closeted in
and my breath won't come.
Pop takes my hand.
His hand, callused and strong,
his chin good and solid,
Pop Van Winkle
gone, like in a long, long sleep,
but here he is back with me.

So with my other hand
I clutch comic books and magazines to my chest.
The ones I have brought for Redbud.
I can think of nothing else
and now in this hall, too,
thinking, I have got to get
these to Redbud.

I see Pop's watch. Twelve-thirty.
Lunchtime. Will they even let us in?
I move ahead of Pop,
walking fast.
The counter stops me.
It does not stop Pop.
He talks in whispers
to the volunteer ladies.
His hands moving.
I follow as they walk.
A tight hold
on the magazines.
We are in the elevator.
Pop waves thank you, harder
than he has to,
to the ladies

who give their permission.
We travel past the second,
third and fourth floors.
At the top floor
we trip over each other
scrambling for the nurses' station.
The nurse smiles.
Pop nods, smiles big.
We breeze past
to find windows with doors
that lead to more windows,
where I see sick people now.
Pop takes me to one window that
I see in to a small figure
wrapped like a cocoon not moving.
Not a peep from him,
not a wink.

How I wish we could go
backward in time
to when he was himself
and I was myself.

And I am crying again,
almost screeching like before.

And Pop, he looks at me
as if he has just read my thought.
"Oh, Ceil," he says.
"No. No.
He's not dead. He's sleeping.
Now you listen.
You hearing me?"
I shake my hair and head, yes.
"He will be well.
They need to keep
him warm.
Give him food.
He can't take it himself.
But he's alive,
and he is breathing.
Watch."
I look
through the window
to the nubby blue blanket that rises, then falls.
My mouth is on the window.
I cannot go into his room.
I have said nothing but he understands
and takes the comics and magazines.
The ones I bring him because if only he reads enough,
fills up with all those words

about Spider-Man,
and fishing,
he will never
have anything bad happen to him again.
With all that information
how could anybody help but stay safe?
And I am the one giving it to him.
Helping to keep him safe.
Will I be forgiven, then?
Do I even get a second chance?

I take to cleaning the mini-blinds,
wiping mirrors clean,
bleaching the counters.
Pop tells me "Here, Ceil, like this.
Put a little elbow grease into it.
That's how your gran showed me."
But when he tells me this
he seems rushed
and worried.

I think Pop is maybe still a little afraid of Gran.
Gran's love does not mean egg on the counter,
a raggedy hem,
or bangs below the eye.

Gran's love comes neat as a pin.
When I ask him why Gran stays up North,
not coming here to live near us,
Pop raises his eyebrows the way he
always does at the mention of the North.
Like it is a whole 'nother planet of its own
beyond anybody here in Texas's understanding.

The doorbell rings and it's May
come to say how sorry she is
and to give me a little green greeting card
with pony stickers inside
that I will not stick to my journal,
but my geography notebook,
and my forehead if I want.
She is sad for me,
kind of sniffling.
I sniffle back,
until we are holding
each other,
and our shoulders are shaking,
feeling miserable
and good with each other.

She can't help it when she has to leave.
Her daddy, in his white pickup truck,
waves to me,
to show me he, too, cares, a little.
She can't help it that
when she walks away her sweater shimmers in the sun-
    light.
Her hair is so clean and blond
it shines and bounces in the way only
hair rinsed that squeaky clean can.
She can't help it
that before she is even at the curb
and stepping into that safe truck,
she has lifted her shoe to wipe the sandy dirt off.

I figure if I keep busy
I will have no time to think
on how things could have been different.
How I could have kept him safe.
I am cleaning like this
when I remember
visiting hours at the hospital are between two and four.
"Pop, Pop, I've got to go now!"
And I do get these words out

and Pop looks at me like I am all new,
not the girl I am here right now
with a half-shirt tied at my ribs,
jeans shorts
almost to my knees,
my hair mucky,
but he looks at me as if
I have a new dress on, a new hairdo,
new everything.
But it's only that I have said something.
I am talking!
And it's like I have come to life.
I discover something just then.
It's words, not breathing,
that bring us to life.
Redbud has been moved
out of intensive care
and onto the second floor,
where he is showing "remarkable improvement,"
by all that the chart at the information booth
says, read by two ladies helping each other.
Ladies with rosy cheeks and bright eyes,
helpful, hopeful faces,
who do not know my friend, at all.
So why do they pretend?

When I walk toward his room
I am shivery with excitement.
Improvement.

Pop takes his time,
still behind me grabbing coffee
at the machine in the waiting room.

In the corner of Redbud's room,
room 161,
as I enter I see
just out of the reach of the overhead light the sergeant
    major,
standing, head down, hands clasped in front,
wearing a red baseball cap.
Can't make out his eyes.
I see two lines on his face
drawn as if by tears.
A broody mouth.
He looks up at me.
I smile.
He looks down again.
Very sad, I think.
I venture into the room
and ask, "How are you?"

"I don't guess very good," he says.
"Someday, Cecelia, you need to tell me all about it.
    Hah!"

Then the light, the bluish, inky fluorescent light
touches his upturned face.
His mouth a hole.
His eyes like sockets
or gargoyle gods',
his lids like pennies closing them off.

I leave the room.
Got to get Pop.
He is unwrapping
a peppermint candy,
sticking it in his mouth,
when I run up to take his hand like I used to,
that hand that has seen me through
nighttime prayers,
riding a two-wheel bicycle,
and Christmas afternoons.

"Redbud's dad is here."
And I guess Pop can just see what it is I don't say,
that Redbud's dad is here

and he is really scaring me.
Pop spits the peppermint
in the ash bucket.
He grips my hand
and walks me into the room,
Redbud's room.
"Where is he?" Pop asks.
Because a woman is in there taking notes.
"This child's dad?" she asks,
pointing to the bed, which is empty now.
Which is what I noticed right off.
"Yes," Pop says, looking at the bed. He is uneasy.
"Signing papers," she says.
Then she sticks her hand out to Pop.
"My name is Paula Fountain.
I am Redbud's caseworker.
Redbud is in therapy.
We are moving him home next week.
The family and I."
She moves to look at me
because I am still not all the way inside the room.
She says, "An accident is really beyond anyone's control,
even yours, Cecelia."
She smiles
like she has known me.

But she does not know me,
and I do not return her smile.

"Of course I will continue
my periodical visits to his home.
We will help you take care of your friend, Cecelia."
And I can see that she means that.
I smile, then, a half-smile.
"Is that okay with you, Cecelia? Cecelia?"

Pop asks me later, at home over a TV dinner,
why I did not answer her.
I tell him I did not hear her.
He says, "What was it was botherin' you then?"
I say, "I don't know."
But I do know.
We are moving him home in a week.
Periodical visits.
Periodical visits are just that, periodical,
and sounding like some geographical magazine bought
   from McCleary's Drug Store for $2.00 apiece,
or something to do when you absolutely have to,
must see to.
Not something done with regularity,
with safety in mind.

Then Pop tells me Auntie is coming
to stay the night.
"Just you ladies," he says with awkwardness.
Giving away the fact
he has no clue
about us ladies.
Still it is good to be home
here, where I watch Sis take to doing my chores.
Chores I don't need to do for this one night.
We take to calling it my night.
Cecelia's night.
I eat juicy apples,
and corn bread and chili,
enjoying Pop more than usual,
who is at home,
not with the yellow birds.
Keeping me close, instead.
And I have to wonder,
were they absent after all or was I, really?
I had gone into myself.
To be in a separate place.

Auntie Lidia braiding my hair,
curls she can't capture

drift into my ears, tickling.
Auntie Lidia is so pretty.
All eyelashes and sweet-smelling skin.
Not honeysuckle but lavender.
Not like my mother.
My mother did not belong to my pop
the way Auntie Lidia does to Uncle Troy,
but this is okay tonight because
this is just what I believe I need.
"Find a nightgown, Cecelia," Auntie says,
"one from Gran."
Behind my bedroom door
my nightgowns are in a nest
of flower prints and small bows.
Tonight as I sliver into one
I feel protected and comforted.
And Auntie combs my hair out like silk, like hers.
And she yawns and whispers,
"Ceil, why, don't you look lovely. Like a princess."
She fans the mirror in front of me.
And I do.
And that is okay tonight, too.
I don't usually like the princess idea,
but tonight being a princess feels okay,
for just this one night.

And she has lit a candle
and has the playing cards out
and we play Crazy Eights
in our pajamas
and talk and when Sis joins us,
I smile and think they look
alike, Auntie Lidia and Sis,
both soft and pretty.
But I am not alike.
I am pretty, I guess,
but not too pretty.
I am soft, too, I guess,
but not too soft.
It's like they have no knots in their hair ever
or warts on their hands.
Heaven forbid if a wart
so much as crept close to Sis.
She never held my warty hand ever, ever.

It was Mom who held it, cleaned it, then removed it with
Wart-Off, and cleaned the blood off with a tissue,
saying, "My, my, a wart the size of a peanut.
I believe you have some kind of record for that one."
Smiling, laughing, hair never in place, my mama.

"Ceil." Pop sees my new hairdo, my blue cotton night-
    gown.
He has come in to say good night to us all.
To peek in, as he says.
But tonight he is all the way in the room
and he is seeing me and saying,
"My, but you look like your mama."
And I don't say a thing, I am
busy being seen by him,
his eyebrows like ragged mustaches,
his uncertain brown eyes,
not like the sergeant major's,
not even shining,
but for seeing
into mine, deep seeing,
and tonight it fills me up
like when I was littler with my mama,
on her lap,
in her arms,
him there loving us.
Not since she left
had he looked at me like that.
Not since she left
did I ever feel that way again,
full and happy,

better than a spoon full of sugar
or sun-warm strawberries,
his look was.
And now he has tears in his eyes
and I do, too,
and then everybody does
and I guess some of these tears
are for my mama and me,
and some for Redbud,
and Sis is crying and Auntie
and Pop he holds me
whispering, "I am sorry, Ceil,
I expected you to be the sky and hold
all of us in your beautiful blue eyes, baby,
but I did no work,
only in my own garden.
I let you down."
"Okay, Pop," I say. "It's okay."
"No, I have a lot to make up for."
And he does, we both know it.

Pop's car,
not the truck.
A pink number
but not froufrou pink.
A splash of grapefruit-juice pink.
His silver-chrome Thunderbird.
Very polished.
Inside, it smells of cucumbers.
Snapping fresh.
Roomy.
We drive the street.
It is like I have never seen this street before.
It just keeps opening up
to let us pass.
It opens up further
to let us go fast.
"Feel that wind, Cecelia."
With my head out the window,
I watch myself

in the side-view mirror,
making a face I hope
is ugly as a troll.
I look up at the sky,
so blue, blue.
I surprise myself
back in the mirror
with a smile.
I duck my head back inside the car
and cross my arms,
saying, "How much longer?"

We are going to Redbud's,
after Pop told me at the breakfast table,
"A kid can't do it alone, Ceil.
It takes a parent helping.
Best if one of their own,
but does not need to be."

I said okay.
It is really okay
with Pop beside me.
Pop here for me
and for Redbud.

We turn in the driveway,
where I see Maggie
still tied to the pole.
She looks hot.
The Cadillac is in the drive,
but the Chevy pickup is not.
I see the same pitched rocking chair,
crumbling chimney.
"An old woman of a house," Pop says,
setting the parking brake.
"In need of fixing."

I watch Pop,
watch his eyes,
his firm mouth.
He is not afraid.
I hop out of the car
running.
Redbud.
Pop is calling behind me,
"Hello? Hello!"

Redbud's memaw
comes from round the back of the house.
She holds pansies

in one hand, a spade in the other.
From under a sun visor her lips move, asking,
"Yes?"
"Redbud, is he up?" I ask.
"No. He needs sleep," she says,
then looks down at her pansies.
Pop says, "Those flowers are wonderful hardy."

"Yes, well. Been hot here for April," she says,
looking away toward the yard.
"But they are a lively flower." He says
it gently with his brown eyes searching,
for hers under that visor.
"If you'd like, Cecelia and I will help you plant those.
Until the boy wakes."

"Until wha . . . ? I suppose . . ." Then she smiles, says,
"Are you thirsty?"
"Could do with a sip of lemonade."
Memaw smiles. "Come on in."
She climbs the stoop slowly.
"Ah, my legs. They don't carry me so well anymore."
Pop takes her elbow and eases her up the steps.
"I make the coldest lemonade this side of Fort Worth,"
    she says.

Inside, Pop introduces himself as Theodore.

Theodore?

She is Laura.

Laura?

She looks like Redbud.

Same brown eyes.

Same soft smile.

Wonder why I never saw this before.

She pulls the ice tray from out of the freezer,

grabs a dish towel off the sink

and begins sweeping it across the counter.

Bread crumbs form in a clump that she

palms, then shakes open-handed into the trash canister.

"I've got to clean this mess up."

She smiles back at us as she says and does it.

"Always like this, the counters.

Leastways till now.

The sergeant major is gone.

Redbud's daddy.

You may know him or of him."

She turns looking at Pop and then me.

"Job hunting out of state.

Something promising."

She says this like she does not really care

if he ever comes back. Gone. Gone like so many bread
   crumbs.

I edge off the chair between whiffs of conversation,
saying, "I'll just go check."
I tiptoe down the hall but land with a thump at his door.
I want him to know I am coming.
I open his door and peek in.
I can't find him for the quilt, flowers, and fruit baskets.
All from Sara Church Home.
Little note tags tied to each one,
with sayings on them.
Chirpy Chipmunk wants you chipper soon.
From all of us to y'all!
Snatches of names scribbled on the insides of the notes,
Hanna, Sue, Kathy,
Paula Fountain.

A fly buzzes past me out the door.
"Buddy?" I whisper.
"Huh? Scout?"
"Yes!"
"Go away! I want to sleep.
I don't need a magazine on Alaska, Madagascar,
or the wallaby in Australia. I don't even want Spider-Man.

I need sleep."
"Who says?" I ask.
"Not allowed."
"Who says?" I ask again.
"Doctor's orders," he says.
"But you have a chair on the porch.
I can take you out. They wouldn't
have got you a wheelchair to ride in
if you couldn't go for a ride,
now would they?"
He doesn't say a word.
That is when I wonder if he is holding on to a grudge.
His head might not always hurt.
His knees heal,
and legs,
but can he forgive me?

His legs won't go in the shorts
that he tries to tug
over his pajama bottoms.
"I'll do it. I'll do it," I say.
"I'll do it, Scout."
And somehow he does not seem like the boy
I can tug pant legs onto anymore.
He is still serious,

but there is more to him,
more solid,
and careful,
and knowing.
I ask his memaw and
my pop,
"Can we go? Huh? Yes?"

"Yes, yes, we'll catch up with you two.
But stay close to the road.
It'll be easier to push that contraption."
And I have already grabbed two bent fish poles
and a tackle box.
I hand them to Redbud to hold.
I push him to the boardwalk
to fish the lotus pond.
Lotus being about as foreign here
as rainbow trout,
but not really,
because they are
speckling everything.

I push him over the rickety boards
of the walkway,
past the branches, and over stones and sticks.

One stick I believe is a snake,
another a giant water bug.
And I am scared, scared something will happen to him
    again,
which means I am scared of almost everything.
Like when my mom died,
at night I checked my closet for witches and
swore that ghosts visited me,
moving my toothbrush from the spot I had marked
with a sticky red star.
Next morning finding my toothbrush moved,
or at least not still on the star.
Being afraid of dying in a way other kids never
think about.
Being different.
That is what I loved Redbud for.
Different but never shying away from that.
Always going for the truth.
Fearless.
Fearless.
I breathe in, then out.
And I do get him to the dock because I have to,
where there are rails to guard him if need be,
and a bench to sit on,
and the water is calm,

calming me.
And I ask him after his first cast
and mine, too,
after we do not snag our lines on lotus pods,
or pond weed.

"How did you learn to fish that way?"
"What way?" he says, seeming to worry over his line.
"You, well, feel for the fish."
"A long way back I learned it."
And that was all he would say, so I let it alone.

"A fish, you know, if it's sly," he starts,
"will nibble at the bait.
A really smart one can nibble it off the hook
without you or me even knowin' it.
I learned to fish with my dad.
Back when he was at Fort Hood.
We fished sometimes from a bridge.
Sometimes from shore.
He learned to fish from his daddy,
my granddaddy.
Fish quiet and steady.
Cast with one smooth action.
Mostly he showed me how to snag it.

To feel the first strike. Let that one go.
The second, too. But on the third you set the hook.
Usually that's right. And usually it's a big one.
One that's been in these waters longer."
"Could you teach me to fish like that?" I ask.
He turns to the river and says something.
"What?" I ask.
"I am teaching you. All along I have."

I feel the tug on my line, then. The first hit.
What if I don't set the hook in time?
And those sticks, the line could snag.
And I need to miss those low branches.
"I do not want to lose this fish," I tell him.
Like the lost catfish.
How is one supposed to get used to losing so much?
A mother, a father's love,
a sister's sisterliness.
Shutting things out, that is how.
I cannot do a thing.

"Scout, it's like this,
you don't think,
you go with the current
and trust it.

Even my daddy knew that
once."

I remember, then,
on one of my visits
to Redbud's.
In his closet,
that army uniform
Redbud keeps for the sergeant major.
He told me, "I'm keeping it for him, in case."

And I knew what he meant by in case.
In case the sergeant major
didn't go looking for that job,
telling them all
he would rather be anywhere but with them,
always something better out there,
the next state, next town, next what else?
He closeted up his courage like that uniform
as Redbud faces it all head-on
in school, the shame of being treated so badly at home.
His ragged jeans, too close-cropped hair.
That wide grin that might as well say kick me.
Go ahead, I will let you.
But he does his duty.

Every day he goes to school and gets good grades.
But the sergeant major put it away, that uniform,
his duty to his family.
He must love his son, I think,
but maybe he lacks the courage.
He needs to wear that uniform every day
or what it stands for.

And I think then about Redbud.
That word I know my mother would have had for him—
    sincere. Meaning, according to the Webster's, pure,
    genuine, *true*.

I forgot about my own truth
when I yelled at him so,
forgot the lightness between us,
who we were with each other,
but he did not, he never does.
It's almost as if he knows something
no one else does.
That maybe there is more to this life
than blame, and anger, good and bad.

Like that bobber in the middle of the water,
rising and falling and rising again

on top of the water.
To stay afloat,
no matter what.
The courage that took.

"Look! You got it!"
He wrangles it.
I move to grab the line.
Bring the fish in for him.
He almost glides
in front of me,
and then he is standing there
at the water's edge,
the edge of the dock,
the railing,
between him and the biggest catfish
I've ever seen come out of the Trinity.
"Wahoo! Scout!
I am bringing it out!"

And it is too big, he decides,
then goes to throw it back,
but it just slips from his hand and into the water.
"Well, that fish knows its way back home," I say.

I hear the brush move,
then Pop and Memaw clip-clopping along the bridge.
The sunlight bright behind them,
Memaw's laughter.
This is how it is for her
without the sergeant major.
Sunlight and laughter.
He is her son.
Redbud is her grandson.
To choose?
Questions again.
Sometimes you just have to let it be.
Sunlight and laughter.

I look to Redbud,who is already back in the wheelchair,
    to answer.
I do not want to give away
that he was standing and fishing.
That's for him to do.
But all he has to say is "No need to push me anymore.
I can do it."

It is agreed we will stop back.
I will give Redbud yet another comic,
and I know it is to check on Redbud.

Pop will not have that talk with the sergeant major yet.

He says to me later that things seem to be going pretty
   well.

But Pop's eyes say something else.

Pop never tosses a thing over in his mind just once.

Maybe that's why he's in a cloud half the time.

He thinks deep on things.

And I know he is studying Redbud's home in his mind,

maybe wondering, too, where the caseworker,

Paula Fountain, is off to.

In the Thunderbird

on the ride back home,

I ask, "Pop, remember you said

there are worse things

than not being able to walk?"

"Yes," he says, "being able to walk

but living like you can't."

"Yes," I say, then I watch out the window,

spying a roadside picnic table,

stony creek bed,

and water unfold like a blue ribbon.

I look back at Pop fiddling with the radio knobs.

This is a big car, I think.

How hard it must be

to keep it straight
to know just when to turn
and when not to.
Pop can do all that and sing, too.

A cloud is hanging and haunting Redbud's house
when I walk through the door of wasps
and into the musty kitchen.
I have seen the Chevy truck in the drive.
It does not take me by surprise.
I knew he'd be back.
Nodding to Memaw, who has opened the door for me,
I spy a comic book lying open on the kitchen table.
It is one of *my* comics,
and as I hand her another,
I am glad that somebody is reading them.

"He is in his room," she says. "Go on now.
He'll be glad to see you."

As I walk down that long hallway
cigarette smoke drifts
in from the outside.
I keep going,
my legs take me

all the way past the orange-smelling room
into Redbud's bedroom
where my lavender water that I sprayed
on my wrists and waist the way Auntie Lidia
does, drifts up to me with the draft from the door.
Before I spy Redbud I see myself
in his long mirror.
My hair in a braid
held at the end with one of Aunt Molly
who-lives-in-Ireland's hair combs.
I have my flip-flops on.
The ones with an orange daisy
like a big orange button at the center of each one.

We play a game of Fish on Redbud's bedroom floor,
where he lies shuffling cards.
Maggie is sniffing the water glass beside him.
"Smells my peanut butter
from this morning's toast," Redbud says
with a snort of laughter,
then he pushes a card at me.
Before I can grab it
I've gone and knocked over that glass of water.
It is as I am wiping it with a sheet
that I see the sergeant major's boots,

black ones
with steel toes.
I look up at his face,
no smile there,
eyes like matchsticks on fire.
I don't know why but I'm mad
at those boots
in front of me.
"Yes, sir?" Redbud says.
Then I see that Maggie is licking up that water.
"I tol' you she's an outside dog. I tol' you that!
How many times I got to tell you!"
He swings wildly at Redbud with his open palm.
"Yes, sir. I'm taking her out now, sir."
Redbud slides in front of me, acting like a shield,
but when he does he coughs a little.
The sergeant major and I both know he is not yet
able to take the dog outside.
"Gimme that leash. You idiot."
And now I'm really mad.
And I swipe at that water,
attacking it, to get it all up
off the wood floor
before Maggie—
just get her out of the way, I think,

out of harm's way.
But as I do, those boots land in the middle of the sheet
so when the sergeant major goes to move
he trips.
Maggie scampers.
And I am not exactly smiling,
but a little.
"Think you're so smart, do you, missy?"
As he catches himself from falling
then catches my wrist in his ivory-hard hand.
And before I know it he has me
standing up in front of him
and all I can do is watch the wrist
that he dares take hold of.

But this, too, does not surprise me.
I have been thinking all along,
something like this could happen to me.
Why wouldn't it?
I entered this house insisting it was okay,
but knowing in that piece of my mind
that it was not.
"How 'bout I take and send you packin'?
Think you're so smart, missy."

He is strong.
His forearm twisted like a singed log.
I can't breathe.
Walls closing in—
but not so close anymore,
not blinding me as in the past.
I see him all right.
I look right into those eyes,
more bloodshot than fiery,
like he's been drinking.
A smile to show his gums.
His barrel chest heaving.
A tiny vein throbbing in his cheek.

"Leave Cecelia alone, Pa," Redbud says.
"What! You boy!"
Redbud is at his closet,
opens the door,
and that same uniform is hanging there.
Bright bronze star.
Collar crisp. Army olive.

Redbud is standing up and facing the sergeant major,
his little bony legs locked tight,
his hand at his brow in a salute.

He salutes him, his daddy.
Even the sergeant major is stopped by this sight
of Redbud skinny as a cornstalk,
swaying, sweating, one hand holding the bureau top,
the other rigid and firm.
And he is firm
like when he fished
steady and sure,
and I know Redbud will never give up,
he would take an arrow for me,
I knew that back when,
I know it now,
and I know the sergeant major knows, too.
And what can any form of hate do to
someone with that kind of courage?
He knows that, too.
So he does not salute back.
He shrugs his shoulders,
no longer pulling on my arm.
I move toward the door
as he walks to the uniform,
not wanting or not choosing to do more,
but losing Redbud in that moment.
Leaving him there with the uniform,

his hand running along the red, black,
green and gold ribbons,
we get out of that place
to where Memaw has the door open for us
and as she guides us past,
and Maggie, too, there with us,
I am remembering Laura
with the soft brown eyes
and cold, cold lemonade.
She winks at me,
as she helps Redbud into the backseat
of her old Cadillac.

Rain beats on the car roof and hood
like my breathing,
fast and hard.
But then as we sweep along the dusty road
my breathing is soothed by the
wishy-washy of the windshield wipers,
the steady speed of tires on pavement,
the music Memaw has on the radio,
trumpet music, jazz,
and I know it to be an old, old song.

I see the white Trinity.
A slow, take everything into it kind of river.
It is white because the clouds
also settle into it,
not on it.

We are back to where we started,
passing where I know the thrumpity old bridge
to be, there behind the trees.

Only Redbud tells me it's not thrumpity
at all anymore, but like cement.
"Nails!" Redbud says, pointing
to it, nails that have been hammered,
holding the bridge secure.
"I wish it would sway," he says.
"I wish we had a rope to cling to, there," I say.
"And a rushing river to swing out over," he says.
We are snug like this in the backseat,
all the way home playing our game.
"And fish the size of dolphins!"

Next time I see him is not at school.
From the other kids' whispers,

and then Pop's kindly voice, I hear
he is back at Sara Church Home,
where Memaw brought him that same rainy afternoon
in her Cadillac.

But today he came for me
with Maggie and her pup,
and after we walk in silence
broken only by scampering dogs,
we are at the river,
where we set our fish poles,
sit back and have a talk.

"Scout," he says, "a trailer on Lake Granbury.
Just me and Memaw and our dogs.
In this great trailer with a dock and all."

But why so far?

"We have to sell our house.
A trailer is what we can afford."
"But what about your dad?"
Redbud does not look down, but directly at me.
"He is going away. Found that job."

And I know it is because there is nothing for him here.
No way he can go back to the old ways.
And really that job was most important after all.

I will miss Redbud.
Fifty miles away being more like five hundred.
And as I wait on the shore alongside him,
he looks bigger now.
Our poles side by side on the dock.
"This is something we share," I say.

The look he gives me I'll remember always,
just as I will this day.
His thin back, arm raised up,
a splash of the bait hitting the water,
his smile, when he turns.

When I go home
Auntie Lidia is on the bench swing.
"Come sit beside me, Cecelia," she calls out.
When I sit next to her
I smell her lavender water,
and something else she has on,

maybe her soap,
and the rosebush with the pink roses
under the front window,
I smell it, too.
My toes won't touch the red dirt
no matter how hard I try to get them to.
Auntie Lidia has a journal
on her lap. Her handwriting
a vine along the white page.
And when she takes my hair in her hands
and begins to loosely braid, she says,
"You're warm, baby,"
and then sweeps my brow with her palm,
puts her arm around me
and we quietly swing,
her chin meeting my forehead. Bone to bone.

I hear the sounds of Pop cooking dinner inside.
The clanging of pans,
the little *chop, chop, chop*ping he does
with the onions.
And then I remember,
it is Saturday and it will be hamburger casserole tonight.
Tonight when Uncle Troy brings

Aldo back from his Saturday soccer game.
And I sure hope he has won,
because if his team lost
he will gripe all the way till next Saturday.

His Halloween sign is in the yard.
He has hammered it in at the front walk.
ENTER IF YOU DARE
"Same old Aldo," I whisper.
I am glad for it.
The sameness.
The regular hum of our house.
No shadow questions
of gargoyles or gods.

Then there is a whir of an engine
down the road.
I look for Uncle Troy and Aldo to pull up.
It is Sis 'n' Eddie who pull up
in Eddie's white CJ5 Jeep.
And then I know what it feels like
to be really glad to see your sister.
She and Eddie come up the walk
laughing, take one look at us

and say, "Oh!"
as if they are one person,
and surprised by us.

I slip from the swing to burrow
between them.
We all three climb the porch steps
to the hall upstairs.
I hear Pepe rustling to catch up.
Eddie holds my arm saying,
"Wait'll you see what we got at the mall."

I'll be right there,
I tell him, but
first I go into the bathroom
to wash my face
with cool, bubbly water.
It's when I look up
that the mirror opens up
and on the other side is me,
and it is enough.

ABOUT THE AUTHOR

Christine Ford grew up in the beautiful Berkshires in western Massachusetts. She now lives in Texas, close to the Trinity River, on which Fort Worth was established. She is a graduate of the University of Utah. Christine Ford likes to write poetry and is often inspired by the beautiful places where she has lived. She is a member of the 4 Star critique group in Fort Worth. This is her first novel.